RUSTLERS' BEND

Center Point
Large Print

**This Large Print Book carries the
Seal of Approval of N.A.V.H.**

RUSTLERS' BEND

WILL ERMINE

CENTER POINT LARGE PRINT
THORNDIKE, MAINE

This Center Point Large Print edition is published
in the year 2015 by arrangement with
Golden West Literary Agency.

The text of this Large Print edition is unabridged.
In other aspects, this book may vary
from the original edition.
Printed in the United States of America
on permanent paper.
Set in 16-point Times New Roman type.

ISBN: 978-1-62899-395-0 (hardcover)
ISBN: 978-1-62899-399-8 (paperback)

Library of Congress Cataloging-in-Publication Data

Ermine, Will, 1888–1979.
Rustlers' Bend / Will Ermine. — Center Point Large Print edition.
pages ; cm
Summary: "Sheriff Farraday will risk everything to stop a gang of
murderers and rustlers"—Provided by publisher.
ISBN 978-1-62899-395-0 (hardcover : alk. paper)
ISBN 978-1-62899-399-8 (pbk. : alk. paper)
1. Large type books. I. Title.
PS3507.R1745R87 2015
813'.54—dc23
2014037699

RUSTLERS' BEND

Chapter One

THE DEAD WITNESS

No one expected the inquest into the death of Jeff Foraker to produce any new evidence. It was well known that the man, one of several thousand who had flocked to the new gold diggings in Rustlers' Bend, had been murdered and robbed of the gold he was carrying.

Foraker's friends had noted his disappearance, and after several days of searching Deputy Sheriff Jim Lord had discovered the riddled body beneath a pile of dead sage a short distance off the road between Rock Creek and the Bend.

The proceedings in the basement room of the courthouse were brief. The four-man jury put their heads together, and after some whispering Coroner Shep Failes announced the verdict.

"The deceased, Jeff Foraker, came to his death by reason of gunshot wounds inflicted by a party, or parties, unknown."

That was all, and Sheriff Kize Farraday snorted contemptuously as he filed out of the room with Lord and Otis Longyear, the district attorney.

"Hell's fire!" old Kize growled. "What's the country comin' to, when you got to waste time and taxpayers' money on such nonsense? It don't make Jeff Foraker no deader than he was when Jim found him."

Longyear nodded his agreement. "It just makes him legally dead," he said with a smile. He was as young as Kize was old and frankly ambitious for himself. Since Rock Creek had gone mad with the stampede to the diggings at Rustlers' Bend, a dozen miles north of town, robberies and murders had been multiplying. According to the official records, Jeff Foraker was the seventh man to be foully done away with. That there were others of whom the law had no record was hardly to be questioned.

"Have you and Jim dug up anything new?" Longyear asked, and his tone was sober enough now.

"Yeh, but nothin' that you'd call important." Kize shook his head. "It has to do with some more of them 'parties unknown' that Shep mentioned. You ain't interested in what you call my hunches, Otis; you want indisputable facts and evidence that'll stand up in court. This may git to that, but I ain't figgerin' on makin' any arrests in the next five or ten minutes."

There was a mild rebuke in his words. Jim Lord knew that Kize intended there should be. With the general public—and the county commissioners in particular—demanding that something be done to check the mounting wave

8

of lawlessness, Longyear, mindful of his own interests, had been putting increasing pressure on the sheriff. Lord saw the young D.A.'s head go up an inch or two, proof enough that he had caught the sting in Kize's remarks.

"You're welcome to your theories and hunches." The glance that Longyear laid on old Kize was definitely hostile. "They're a mighty poor substitute for action, with things going from bad to worse every day."

Otis Longyear was only twenty-nine. For twenty-eight of those years Kize Farraday had worn the silver star that adorned his vest this morning, worn it in a way to win the respect of good men and bad. He didn't relish being told off by a Johnny-come-lately like young Otis. Not that Kize was standing on his past laurels, for, though he was worn and battle-scarred, his indomitable spirit had lost none of its fighting edge.

In the long ago, when rustling had been a recognized business in this section of Nevada and the big bend of Rock Creek had, with good reason, been dubbed Rustlers' Bend—it was the handy back door to the comparative safety of the Snake River Plains for those who swung the wide loop—he had fought range outlawry to a standstill. Even those critics—Otis excepted—who found fault with him today could only say that he was old, not that his bulldog courage or iron will had deserted him.

"I've had the wolves snappin' at my heels before this," Kize observed as they went up the stairs to the main floor of the courthouse. "You'll git used to it as you grow up. In the meantime if it relieves you any to do a little snipin' at me, go right ahead."

Longyear didn't like it, but he managed a laugh. "No need for you to get your dander up. If you think I've been throwing the prod into you, I can tell you there's a lot of people stepping on my toes, too. I can't go to trial with a theory; I need evidence, and I mean evidence that will lead to a conviction. Things can't go on this way much longer—a dead man for breakfast every other day, one robbery after another, rustling getting a fresh start—and nothing being done about it."

Jim Lord had said nothing, confident that Kize could hold his own with Otis. Jim had come in off the range several years back to become the county's first paid, full-time deputy sheriff. He was a quiet, self-contained, seemingly nerveless man, with a pair of gray eyes that had a way of demanding and getting the truth wherever he sought it.

Longyear got along with him well enough, due in no small measure to the fact that he was careful never to step across the line with Lord, either in his official capacity or privately, as he felt free to do with old Kize.

Most of the county offices were located around

the main floor rotunda. As the three men stood there briefly Longyear's quick glance ran from the sheriff to Jim and back to the old man. Believing he was on safe ground and wanting to make sure that he had not come off second best in his tilt with the sheriff, he said, "I know you, Kize. Once you get a bone in your teeth you won't let go. I suppose you've got hold of something that tends to bear out your theory that what we're up against is a syndicate of criminals." His scoffing tone eloquently expressed what he thought about that idea.

"It don't tend to do nothin'; it proves it!" Kize declared hotly. "I been tellin' you for weeks that we're dealin' with an organized ring. Every one of these killin's was planned and carried out according to orders. That's why there's never any evidence left for us to find. That goes for the robberies and the rustlin' and all the rest of it. You can laugh it off, but you'll be laughin' out of the other side of yore mouth one of these days, my boy."

Kize could be patronizing, too.

"I may be young, but I'm old enough to have my eyes open," the district attorney retorted. "A hundred blacklegs and no-goods must have drifted into town since the stampede got going. It's downright nonsense for you to go on insisting that they're all banded together, with a little inner circle pulling the strings. When you first

11

mentioned the idea I thought you were only stalling for time. I played along with you for a while; I knew we had to save face some way. We can't buy any more time with it, Kize; time is something we've run out of. Why don't you get wise to yourself? You know this fellow Jeff Foraker was murdered by someone who was tipped off that the man would be coming in with nine to ten thousand dollars' worth of gold on him. When Foraker was in town last week a saloonful of men heard him say he'd be pulling out for a trip back East to see his people in a few days and that he had leased his claim to Pete and Alf Girard. You heard the marshal testify to that. All the killer had to do was lay out in the hills and watch the road. When Foraker came along he was stuck up and forced out into the brush. It didn't take an organization to pull it off; it was a one-man job."

"You think so, eh?" Kize inquired coolly. There was an obscure light in his faded eyes that boded ill for Longyear. As the saying goes, he had the young district attorney over a barrel now, and he proposed to make the most of it.

Jim Lord knew what was coming, but his lean bronzed face betrayed no sign of it, unless it was an almost imperceptible lifting of the upper lip in a brief and unconscious expression of pity for Otis Longyear in daring to cross swords with old Kize.

"Naturally it's what I think!" Longyear had failed to see the danger signals set against him and rushed in headlong. "Foraker made his mistake in not coming in on one of Mullhall's stages. I suppose he wasn't going to let Wild Bill gouge him out of five dollars for a twelve-mile ride. It would have been five dollars well spent, in his case. I haven't any use for Mullhall and his methods, but his stages are never held up; his drivers know how to shoot, and his shotgun guards learned their business with Wells, Fargo. With that amount of gold on him Foraker never should have come in alone."

Kize gave him a long searching glance that had no mercy in it. Longyear was all right, but he was young, and he had been getting too big for his britches.

"Otis, would it surprise you if I was to say I can prove that Foraker didn't come in alone?"

"No! I can't believe it after what I was told up there yesterday. I—"

"Wal, it's a fact," Kize said flatly. "I've got a witness who will swear under oath that he saw him leave the diggin's with the two companions. The three of 'em went up the trail over the Blue Meadows. That would bring 'em back to the road about a mile above where Jim found the body."

"Can your witness identify the two men who left with Foraker?"

"He says he can identify one of 'em. He ain't shore about the other."

Otis Longyear began to take on a wilted look. Too late he realized that Kize had let him make himself ridiculous. As for Kize, he stood there enjoying his triumph, convinced that there would be no more needling from the D.A.'s office.

The passing years had dried up most of the juices in Kize Farraday. Never a big man, he had shriveled up alarmingly of late until he seemed to be just skin and bones. In jest old cronies had warned him that if he ever got caught out in the open by one of the screaming nor'westers that hit this high country in early winter he'd be swept away like a dancing tumbleweed and end up in some fence corner and not be found till the snow went off the following spring. Not only time but wind and weather had long ago tanned his hide the deep brown of old saddle leather and ground into it an intricate mosaic of lines and wrinkles. With his long scrawny neck, hooked nose, and hooded brows he had something of the look of an old and somewhat moth-eaten eagle, the frosty light in his eyes saying plainly enough that he neither asked nor expected quarter from anyone.

"It's no wonder we're not getting anywhere, with your office and mine working at cross purposes," Longyear burst out in great indignation. "Where do you get the authority to withhold information of this nature from me?"

"Nobody's withholdin' nothin', Otis," Kize returned, completely unabashed. "You been doin' most of the talkin'."

"I'll do some more right now!" the D.A. snapped. "I want you to bring in that man for questioning right away. You know why the commissioners are holding the special meeting this afternoon. We're going to be called in and given a grilling. It may take off some of the heat if we have a lead to talk about. Can you get your man here by one o'clock?"

"No, I wouldn't risk lettin' you question him. And I ain't goin' to disclose his identity, Otis. That was part of the deal I made with him. You didn't git anywheres when you went up to the diggin's and tried to question everyone in sight. There's a feelin' that it ain't safe for a man to come right out and say what he knows. My fella is in town right now. If he spots the parties that was with Foraker he'll git word to me."

"That's interesting—very interesting," Otis acknowledged painfully. He shook his head over the presumed stupidity of Jeff Foraker. "What kind of a fool could Foraker have been? Leaving camp with a couple strangers!"

"What makes you think they was strangers?" Kize demanded.

"You mean they were his friends?"

"I mean they'd been around the diggin's long enough to win his confidence. Foraker was no

15

jackass. By gravy, it's about time you pulled in yore horns, Otis, and listened to me!" Kize had reached the end of his patience. "I told you this proved my contention that this lawlessness is organized. It's as plain as the nose on yore face, if you want to see it. You talk about all the blacklegs that have flocked into town. Of course they're here. But most of 'em are small fry—tinhorns and con men. They'll trim a sucker or roll a drunk, but they ain't killers and road agents or rustlers. The only connection between them and the gents we're after is that they'll keep their mouths shut about anythin' they know. In return the gang tosses 'em some of the crumbs and leftovers. I reckon there ain't more'n twenty men on the inside of the organization. And not all of 'em are hangin' around the saloons in Rock Crick; they got men planted up in the Bend like this pair who steered Foraker to his death. I mean men who're workin' claims, or pretendin' to, and looked on as honest, upright citizens."

Longyear was more impressed than he cared to admit.

"Sounds fantastic to me," he declared, "but I won't argue with you. You may be right. I suppose you've got it all figured out that another bunch of them works the rustling."

"It's bein' done neater than you figger," Kize replied, ignoring the D.A.'s sarcastic tone. "We got a couple thousand more mouths to feed than we had a few months ago. That means more meat. The stock that's bein' run off is bein' slaughtered and sold for beef right under our noses."

"The butchers and the hotel and restaurants know they have to show a hide for every carcass they buy," Otis reminded him. "That's the law. You accusing them of being in on this?"

"No, they can produce the hides. No trick to rewrite a brand, once you've pulled a hide off a cow. No soreness nor anythin' else to give the job away a day or two after it's done."

Longyear didn't know what to say. He turned to Jim. "You see it that way, too?"

"No other way *to* see it," Jim answered. "Under ordinary conditions it would be a cinch to discover who's selling the stuff. But you know things are not normal. Hardly a pound of beef is being shipped in from outside; it's all local meat. With the price sky-high right here in town, every cow outfit around here is trying to grab what it can of the business. When you figure that not more than five percent of the total is rustled stuff you can see what we're up against."

"But how can they work their game without using a registered brand?"

"They got one, Otis!" Kize growled. "Good gravy, they ain't dumb enough to try to slip a strange brand over on us! Someone's thrown in with 'em—somebody who's been runnin' a spread on this range for years. It's jest got to be that way. There ain't no other explanation. Been no transfer of ranch property around here."

"Good heavens!" Longyear got out chokingly. "You mean some respected stockman is a party to all this killing and—"

"That's exactly what I mean!" Kize rapped. "And he ain't no two-bit member either! He'll stub his toe one of these days."

"You got a line on him, Kize?" Longyear was all eagerness now.

"I ain't namin' no names," was the gruff answer. "But I'll crack this thing wide open before I'm through. Jest because Jim and me ain't been ridin' to hell and back and wearin' ourselves to the bone some folks figger we been fallin' down on the job."

Kize snorted contemptuously. Otis Longyear was one of the men he had in mind, and the latter understood that he was included.

"Sometimes there's better ways of catchin' yore crooks than puttin' a shine on the seat of yore britches," the old man observed caustically.

The district attorney had begun seriously to doubt the wisdom of his previous intention to throw Kize Farraday overboard in order to keep himself afloat. The feeling was growing in him that he was going to need Kize, that the old man knew more than he was saying. That a bandit gang was operating at the direction of a key figure no longer seemed incredible.

18

"Don't get me wrong, Kize," he protested. "I rib you a little, but that's neither here nor there; the two of us have got to pull together. I'll let you do the talking this afternoon. What are you going to say to the commissioners?"

"I ain't goin' to say a dang thing! Tell them windbags anythin' and it will be all over the county by nightfall. Don't you start shakin' in yore boots when they begin yappin'. Let 'em threaten all they please. Ain't no one short of the attorney general of Nevada can call us to account. But shucks, I'll set 'em down before they git started. I'm goin' to demand a second full-time depity. That'll cost money, and there ain't nothin' like money to make that bunch start chawin' their whiskers. You run along now and take care of yore business; I got a couple boys in the pokey that ain't had their breakfast yet."

There was a twinkle in Jim's gray eyes when they walked out of the courthouse. "You were a little rough on Otis," he said with a low chuckle. "Are you within your rights in withholding the name of a witness?"

"I don't suppose I am," Kize grumbled. "But Tom Yancey is a good man. He's takin' a chance in comin' through for us. The cat would be out of the bag for shore if it got around that the D.A. had questioned him."

Rock Creek was busier than usual this morning. One of Wild Bill Mullhall's stages

19

rumbled past, its two armed guards unconcernedly maintaining their precarious perch on the roof. Through the dust its passing kicked up, plodded a sixteen-mule team and a string of freighting-wagons bound for the camp at Rustlers' Bend. Thanks to the gold excitement, the town was doing a thriving business. Down in the Nevada and Idaho freight yard a switch engine was noisily shunting cars back and forth.

All this activity was in marked contrast to Rock Creek's placid existence in the days when it was just a sleepy little cow town.

Back in the smoky years when Rustlers' Bend and its midnight riders were something more than just a memory Rock Creek had been little more than a wide place in the road dreaming of the day when the railroad would build up from the south and rescue it from oblivion. The Nevada and Idaho had reached town half a dozen years back. It had given Rock Creek permanence, but, all the previous optimism to the contrary, it had not added materially to its prosperity. It had taken this gold stampede to put the town really on the map. It was what everyone had wanted, but now that it had happened there were those, old Kize among them, who wished devoutly that Jud Hoffsteader had never washed out that first panful of gravel and turned everything topsy-turvy.

It was surface mining—poor man's mining—

and those who might be presumed to know about such things said the gold-bearing gravel would soon be exhausted. Kize recalled the prediction as he watched the heavy freighting-outfit creak by.

"With all them groceries and supplies goin' out, don't look like the camp is goin' to fold up for a while yet," he declared sarcastically. "Wal, see you later, Jim."

He turned the corner for his office and the jail, which were housed together in a small brick building to the rear of the courthouse. Jim started up the street, but not more than a dozen steps separated them when a sharp blast of gunfire brought Kize back on the run.

"What was that?" he whipped out fiercely.

The morning was warm, and the doors and windows along the main street stood open. The rather hollow ring of the shots said plainly enough that they had been fired inside some building.

"Sounded like it came from the Maverick bar," said Jim. The Maverick was Rock Creek's largest hotel. The saloon that was run in connection with it was the most popular emporium of its kind in town.

Though the county sheriff's office was not charged with keeping the peace, that being the responsibility of the town marshal, Kize and Jim headed across the street in the direction of the Maverick on the double-quick. Before they gained the opposite sidewalk a man staggered backward through the swinging doors of the saloon, a wavering gun grasped in one fist and his other hand clutching his throat in a vain effort to stop the blood that was spurting from a ragged wound. Death, not alcohol, was turning his legs to rubber. He half swung around and then toppled over face first on the plank sidewalk and with a last convulsive shudder rolled into the tawny dust of the street.

"My God!" Kize groaned. "It's Tom Yancey! They musta figgered he could identify the two birds who came in with Jeff Foraker!"

"Yeah! And they closed his mouth in a hurry," Jim agreed. "Tom Yancey won't identify anybody for us now. Come on, Kize!"

Chapter Two

DOUBTFUL ALIBI

In the minute or more that it took Kize and Jim to reach the stricken man no one followed him through the swinging doors of the saloon. The usual aftermath of a barroom shooting affray was for those within to come pouring out to see the grim tragedy through to its finish. But not today.

Jim made a mental note of the fact. Considering the hour, he knew the Maverick was far from deserted. Men came running from a dozen other directions, however, as Kize bent down over the huddled form in the dust.

"He's dead!" they heard him say. "Not a twitch left in him!"

Cap Wyeth, the town marshal, was one of the first to reach the sheriff's side. Cap was a round little man, and, though he had barely turned fifty, the exertion of running a block left him panting. In the old days when Rock Creek was just a cow town he had kept the peace in a satisfactory manner, seldom being called on for anything more serious than marching an obstreperous cowboy off to jail. That more or less placid existence had not fitted him to cope with the lawlessness that had begun to run wild soon after the strike at Rustlers' Bend. The town had got away from Cap, and no one knew it better than Jim Lord.

Cap glanced at the dead man and found he knew him only by sight. He managed to catch his breath. "Deader'n a mackerel!" He turned helpless eyes to the sheriff. "Yuh know who got him, Kize?"

Kize was seething. He had counted heavily on the information he believed Tom Yancey would be able to supply. To have the man rubbed out in this fashion was a bitter pill. The marshal's senseless question further infuriated him. He straightened up, bristling.

"You saw Jim and me git here," he snapped. "We was as far away as you when we heard the shootin'." He bore Cap no personal enmity, but it was as plain to him as it was to Jim that the marshal was just a pompous little windbag, hopelessly unfitted for his role of peace officer in a town that had gone hog-wild.

The caustic rebuke having silenced Wyeth, Kize swept the gathering crowd with frosty eyes. Enraged though he was, his cunning did not desert him.

"Any of you boys know this man?" he demanded, indicating the slain miner. He was intent on covering up his connection with Yancey.

"His name's Tom Yancey," one of the crowd

informed him. "He's got a claim up in the Bend."

Kize turned to the marshal.

"Cap, you better find Failes and git his permission to remove the body. We can't leave this man layin' in the road. I'll be inside."

Cap didn't relish being reduced to messenger boy, but, grumbling to himself, he hurried off to find the coroner.

Con Morgan, the proprietor of the Maverick Hotel and bar, pushed through the swinging doors. He was a tall black-haired man with a cavernous face, addicted to brocaded vests of eye-arresting hues. Since he usually went coatless, his weskits were revealed in all their splendor.

Con was not a product of the gold excitement; he had arrived in Rock Creek the year after the railroad reached town, purchased the old hotel, modernized it in many ways, and in five years between then and now established himself as a solid and popular citizen. His reputation having preceded him, he had not arrived in Rock Creek as an unknown. Belmont, the Reese River excitement, Rawhide, and. a dozen other boom towns and gold camps were strung along his back trail. In them he had conducted hotels and saloons and made himself a more or less prominent figure in that segment of Nevada's population that can best be described as drifting. As the expression had it, he was believed to be "well fixed."

What Con had hoped to win for himself in Rock

Creek had never been fully explained. When questioned about it he brushed it aside with the laughing rejoinder that he was fed up with excitement and just wanted to burrow in somewhere, make a living, and "put himself on the shelf."

In the beginning there were some, of course, who suspected that he had had some difficulty with the law and was taking it easy until things cooled off. They said he was a bird of passage and wouldn't remain long. He had proved them completely wrong and so effectively that Rock Creek would have sent him to the legislature had he consented. On the other hand, he had never been able to make the Maverick show a profit. Along with many others he had banked too heavily on what the coming of the railroad was to do for the town. But he had hung on, refusing to believe that the growth and solid prosperity he had envisioned would not materialize eventually. After five years of waiting, however, he was ready to give up when the discovery of gold in Rustlers' Bend changed everything overnight for him.

"Kize, it's a downright shame this had to happen—and in my place." Con shook his head regretfully. "It was a fool play all around. I don't know what got into Yancey. He wasn't drunk. I don't know what he could have been thinking of, drawing a gun on a man."

"You saw the whole thing?" the sheriff demanded.

"Certainly! I was standing right there."

Kize nodded. He had long been on very friendly terms with Morgan and had always found him to be a square shooter. "Who killed him, Con?"

"Chuck Silvey. Yancey didn't leave him any choice about it. Chuck shot in self-defense if ever a man did. You'll find half a dozen boys inside who saw it. They'll tell you the same. There wasn't much of an argument between Chuck and Yancey. Not a dozen words. Chuck and the boys were standing at the bar when Yancey lined up with them. His drink was upset somehow. He accused Chuck of doing it. Chuck called him a liar. Yancey said he'd make him eat it. The next thing we knew, he whipped out a gun. His intention was plain enough. Chuck beat him to it. Come on in," he urged, "and question the boys."

"Just a minute, Con," Jim Lord interjected. He had picked up the gun that had fallen from Tom Yancey's lifeless fingers. "You say this man drew first. His gun hasn't been fired. Strange that with a second or two in his favor he didn't squeeze the trigger. How do you explain it?"

Con caught a vague note of hostility and suspicion behind the question, and he was quick to resent it.

"It ain't up to me to explain anything. I was just telling you and Kize what happened."

"Naturally," Jim agreed. "It just struck me that

27

your friend Silvey must be awfully fast with a gun."

Again Con caught that note of hostility, and not so obscure this time. He smiled, but there was no trace of mirth in his blue eyes.

"Aren't you being a little careless, Jim?" he inquired thinly.

"In what way?"

"Confusing my customers with my friends."

"I didn't mean to be careless," was Lord's soft but pointed answer. "Silvey seems to spend most of his time in your place; if he isn't in the bar you can always find him somewhere around the hotel. If I made a mistake, Con, that's what threw me."

Morgan chose to let it go at that. Jim was content too: he had drawn Con out, and that had been his purpose.

As for Chuck Silvey, he was one of many who seemed to exist without visible means of support. Though he always had money to spend, the only work he did was to fill in occasionally for one of the Maverick's stud dealers. Kize and Jim had long since singled him out for their special attention, but they had never been able to pin anything on him. Killing Tom Yancey had instantly crystallized their suspicions against the man. It found expression in the quick warning glance they exchanged as they followed Morgan into the barroom.

Silvey and the others—eleven in all—lined up against the bar turned to face them. Two or three were men from the diggings; the others were familiar saloon characters and intimates of Silvey. In the rear at a table one of John Woodhull's Double Diamond punchers sprawled in stupefied slumber. Behind the bar the two bartenders gave up their feeble pretense of polishing glasses and came to attention. Kize walked up to Silvey. Jim stopped a few feet away ready to back up any play the sheriff made.

"I told Kize what happened," Con volunteered, "but I reckon he wants to get it firsthand from you, Chuck."

"Sure," Silvey agreed, pushing his hat back on his head and revealing his receding hairline. "There ain't much to tell. You was standing alongside of us. I don't know what I can add to what you saw and heard."

He didn't sound unduly concerned over the fact that he had just killed a man and might find himself in serious difficulty with the law. With consummate nonchalance he proceeded with his account of the shooting, pausing now and then to call on one or another of his cronies to verify some detail. Almost word for word it was the story Con Morgan had told.

Kize prodded him with questions. Jim said nothing. He was convinced that they weren't getting the truth, that the tale had been manufactured. That being true, it followed that Morgan was covering up for Silvey. In itself it posed a whole series of questions that he didn't attempt to answer on the spur of the moment. Instead he continued to watch Silvey closely. He doubted that the man was as shrewd as he appeared. His pronounced lower jaw was wide at the ears and came down in a bold V to end in a pointed chin. Above it a long crooked nose ran up into a slanting forehead, the extent of which was accentuated by his balding head. It gave him a forbidding, wolfish look.

"Give him a chance?" Silvey queried in answer to a question from Kize. "Do you think I was going to stand here and let him plug me? When a crazy fool pulls a gun on you a man's got the right to defend himself. I didn't upset his drink. And what if I had? Was that any reason for him to blow his top?"

"You say you didn't know Tom Yancey," Kize prodded. "You shore about that?"

"Of course I'm sure! I've seen him around town or up at the Bend. That's all. I didn't even know his name. You're barking up the wrong tree, sheriff, if you've got the idea that I ever had any trouble with him. That's what gets me: he didn't have no grudge to settle with me."

Kize realized that he wasn't getting anywhere. He didn't bother to question the others, knowing he would get the same story from them. He would have liked to call Silvey a liar to his face, but he was guileful and held himself in and pretended to be half convinced that he had been told the truth. He turned to Con Morgan.

"His story checks with yours. You ready to take the stand and swear under oath that that was the way it was, Con?"

Con shrugged and fingered the heavy gold watch chain that spanned his ornamental vest. He was wearing a simple—for him—two-toned purple creation bedecked with silver buttons this morning.

"I can only tell it the way I saw it," he said. "I wouldn't give you one story and a jury another."

Kize nodded woodenly. "I figgered you was prepared to go all the way for this fella. I might say it's a considerable favor yo're doin' him. I hope he appreciates it."

Morgan's head straightened up. He didn't like Kize's tone or the implications behind the remark. He regarded him coolly for a moment. "I don't get you," he said with a sharp note of resentment. "Get this straight; I'm not doing anyone a favor. There's half a dozen men here who saw it as I did."

Kize nodded, unperturbed. "I know," he observed pointedly, "but their word don't carry any weight in this town. If Silvey had to depend on them to see him out of this jam he might not git far. It's different with you, Con; if you say it

31

was self-defense, I reckon that's what it will be. If Longyear takes my advice he won't even try to git an indictment."

"If he listens to you he'll save himself some trouble, I reckon," Con declared, his umbrage apparently forgotten. Though he had not expected Kize to admit defeat so readily, he did not question it.

It was different with Jim Lord; he knew Kize Farraday too well to believe for a moment that the killing of Tom Yancey was a closed account in the sheriff's book; he was certain that old Kize had his sights trained on something and was moving toward it with cunning indirection.

"Where do I stand?" Silvey growled. "You takin' me in?"

"No, yo're free to come and go as you please," Kize told him. "If I want you I'll find you." He caught Jim's eye. "Let's git out of here."

Even as he spoke, Wild Bill Mullhall slammed through the swinging doors and strode up to the bar. With a contemptuous disregard for those present he slapped down a silver dollar and struck the polished surface of the bar a resounding whack with his clenched fist.

"Let's have it!" he roared.

An expectant hush had fallen on the Maverick with his coming, and the air was suddenly charged with something electric. Kize instantly gave up any thought of leaving.

Wild Bill's angry bellow had jerked the bartenders out of their momentary trance, and both leaped to do his bidding. He filled a glass to the brim from his favorite bottle and dashed it off neatly. He seemed to enjoy the silence he had produced. With greater deliberation he downed another drink. He turned then and, with elbows cocked on the bar railing, leaned back and fastened his round, venomous eyes on Morgan, Chuck Silvey, and the half-dozen others who traveled with Silvey.

From his sneering, withering scrutiny Kize and Jim, as well as the several miners from the Bend, were definitely excluded. There were devils in Mullhall's eyes. Con stood up to them, but Silvey and his friends shifted about uneasily under their dreadful gaze. They were hard men, some of them with records as long as their arms, but they were novices in violence and gun smoke compared to this man whose deeds had been the subject of awed discussion in every cow camp and mining town west of the Rockies for a decade and more.

He had been called monster and fiend incarnate by many, and by others a brave and fearless champion of law and order. Those who could not condone the methods he used could not deny that in his capacity of division agent for Wells, Fargo he had cleaned up more than one mountain division that had been at the mercy of road agents and outlaws and made them safe for the passage of passengers and treasure. He had killed twenty-nine men, Indians not included, and beaten scores of others into insensibility with his iron fists. It was nowhere of record that any man who had received a beating at Bill Mullhall's hands had ever asked for a second helping.

Drink had been his undoing. In his cups he was a demon, and his lapses had become so frequent that the express company was forced to dispense with his services fifteen months ago. He had dropped out of sight for a time, but word that gold was being found at the grass roots in Rustlers' Bend had reached him, and he had suddenly appeared in Rock Creek with a handful of his followers and captured the freight and passenger business to and from the Bend.

Rock Creek had not yet forgotten the day of his arrival; business had come to a standstill, and miners had laid down their tools and flocked in from the diggings to catch a glimpse of him. All this adulation had been too much for Bill, and he had gone on a drunken rampage, wrecking the Maverick and another saloon before he was through. When he had sobered up he apologized and paid the bill for the damage he had wrought.

Though he was only of medium height, he was built like an oak and possessed the strength of the proverbial bull. Men who had known him in his younger days when he had first hired out to Wells, Fargo as a shotgun guard in Colorado remembered him as a handsome man. No hint of it remained in his beefy pock-marked face today. His wild, uncontrolled temper and drunken debaucheries had stamped it with deeper lines than the passing years, for he was still in his early forties.

Cap Wyeth had walked wide of him from the first. The marshal feared him and made no secret of the fact. He could do it without losing too much face, for the rest of Rock Creek's male population feared him, too. Old Kize was a notable exception. Within a week of Bill's arrival Kize had shown him that he wasn't to be bullied or run over roughshod by anyone. Bill had bought a small ranch two miles north of town and moved his horses and mules there. A county road ran through the property. One morning neighboring ranchers found the road barred with a locked gate. Bill had refused to remove it. Kize had promptly shot the lock off and reduced the gate to kindling wood. Bill had threatened reprisals, but the road had remained open.

The incident had resulted in something approaching mutual respect between them. Though neither cultivated the other, they had become well acquainted with the passing weeks. Kize treated him fairly, did him a favor when possible, and kept an open mind about the man. Wild Bill, for his part, continued his riotous ways, neglecting his business but making money hand over fist, and, though he made trouble for many, he made none for Kize.

If Mullhall was aware of Deputy Sheriff Lord, he never gave any sign of it. What business he had with the sheriff's office was conducted in private with Kize. One morning Jim had over-heard the old man say, "I'll stand for a lot from you, Bill, but it wants to stop short of gunfire." To date it had stopped short of it. It had led Jim to believe that Kize had extracted some sort of a pledge from Wild Bill. He thought of it now and wondered if it explained why the sheriff had so suddenly changed his mind about leaving the Maverick.

By the standards that applied to him Wild Bill was reasonably sober, but he was violently aroused about something, and his whole manner was murderous. When he gave his gun belt a suspicious hitch that brought his silver-handled .45 into easier reach Jim was less than surprised to have old Kize say, "Take it easy, Bill. I'm holdin' you to yore word. No gunplay!"

This forced admission that there was an understanding of a sort between them explained as much to Con Morgan and the others as it did to Jim. Wild Bill's terrible eyes shifted to Kize.

"This comes under the headin' of an exception," he growled. It was his proudest boast that, drunk or sober, he never broke his word. "I just saw Tom Yancey carted away in the undertaker's wagon. Down in Leadville some years ago he did me a considerable favor. I got a long memory for things like that. You let me take this matter off your hands, Kize; I'll square it, and it won't cost the county a cent."

"No," Kize declared adamantly. "You ain't bigger than the law, Bill."

Cap Wyeth and the coroner stepped into the saloon at that moment. What they beheld stopped them in their tracks. They stood there, ignored by all.

"Okay, if that's the way you want it!" Wild Bill rapped. "But, by God, I'll put some teeth in the law!" He swung around on Morgan, Chuck Silvey, and the others, his eyes narrowed to slits. "I heard the talk outside. I want it firsthand now. Which one of you bastards cut him down?"

Con, who had been quick with his story to the sheriff, and Silvey, who had shown no reticence about his part in the shooting, were silent.

"Come on, out with it!" Mullhall ground out. "I ain't askin' how or why. Who got him?"

"I did," Silvey confessed, all his swagger and truculence gone. "I had to drop him. He—"

"Shut up!" Wild Bill growled. "I can figger out the whys and wherefores for myself!" His gaze shifted to Morgan. "You was here. Why didn't you stop it?"

"Why, Bill, I didn't know Yancey was a friend of yours," was the apologetic answer. "I—"

That was as far as he got.

"Well, you know it now! And you know where it puts you with me!"

The blood drained away from Con's face, leaving it pasty and more cavernous than ever. "If you'll only listen, Bill—" he pleaded. Mullhall cut him off fiercely.

"I warned you never to step on my toes! It's too late to come whinin' to me!"

His hand whipped down to his gun. Kize had anticipated the move and was ready for it. He didn't draw, but the advantage was clearly his.

"Forgit it, Bill," he got out grimly. "Don't make me kill you."

Like two graven images they stood there for a long moment, not an eyelash moving.

"I'm damned if you don't mean it," Wild Bill conceded finally. His hand fell away from his gun. "I got no quarrel with you, you spunky little runt. But don't you be surprised if you're sorry one of these days that you stopped me. Don't let 'em tell you Tom Yancey busted in here gunnin' for anybody. They can't hand me that hogwash; he was a peaceable man. He knew somethin'. That's why he was rubbed out. Dead men don't talk. And that goes for dead sheriffs, too. Paste that in your hat and remember it!"

He stamped out of the Maverick, all fire and

fury, shouldering Cap Wyeth out of his way and slamming through the swinging doors so violently that one was left sagging on wrenched hinges.

Kize lingered only until Wild Bill was gone. Then without as much as a glance for Morgan and the others he started for the door. Jim fell in step with him.

The marshal would have stopped them. Kize brushed him aside.

"Yuh shore yuh got all the facts, Kize?" Cap demanded, running after him.

"I got all I'm likely to git—in here," was the sheriff's flinty answer.

Chapter Three

AN UNPOPULAR SHERIFF

"You realize that everything I've said is off the record and strictly between the two of us," Jim Lord observed soberly. "You're free to say what you please about the killing of Tom Yancey, but I don't want you to quote me."

He had just finished giving Iris Farraday, the young and comely editor of the Rock Creek *Enterprise*, a detailed account of what had happened at the Maverick.

"Naturally," Iris agreed. "I'll get something from Dad. Otis will want to make a statement. If I need anything more I can get it from Cap Wyeth. He's always ready to talk if he can get his name in the paper."

The two of them were alone in Iris's private cubbyhole in the *Enterprise* office. The paper was doing well enough now to warrant being published daily. All over Nevada various publications were quoting liberally from its columns. Henry Hustis, the publisher, was making money for the first time in years, and Iris similarly was finding herself a person of some importance. She was a practical young woman, not given to frills. But a plain shirtwaist and tweed skirt could do more for her than evening gowns and diamonds did for many of her sex. It was generally known around town that old Kize was not the only member of the Farraday family for whom Deputy Sheriff Lord had a great admiration.

"What's Dad got to say about it?" she inquired.

Jim shook his head. "Nothing so far. I had just left him down at the office when you tapped on the window and called me in. He told me he wanted to be alone and think things over. He was as cross as a wounded grizzly."

Iris smiled. "He always is when he's got something on his mind." She paused to regard Jim with her dark-brown intelligent eyes for a moment. "What do you make of it?"

"The shooting, you mean?"

"Yes, for one thing."

"I don't know," Jim answered thoughtfully. "Silvey's story is a lie on the face of it. But it's going to be hard to break down; Morgan is ready to back him up, and Silvey had a bunch of his pals on hand to swear it wasn't his fault. The whole thing could have been arranged, and when Yancey walked in Chuck was ready for him."

"But Con Morgan?" she queried. "Why would he be playing Chuck Silvey's game? Is it possible Silvey has got something on Con?"

Jim shook his head again. "I'm not saying what I think."

41

Iris tried to draw him out, but got nowhere.

"Skip it," he said. "It sounds crazy even to me. But it will keep. Con got awfully white around the gills when Wild Bill leveled off on him."

"Bill Mullhall, that exhibitionist!" she exclaimed disparagingly. "I wish Con had called his bluff. I wager Mullhall would have pulled in his horns. You must admit it was a little fishy of him, trying to make an issue out of his alleged friendship for Yancey. I'd be surprised if he even knew the man. Don't tell me you believe it was anything more than a grandstand play."

"Only in the way that everything Bill does is for the grandstand. He likes an audience. But make no mistake about it, Iris; he was ready to kill Morgan and Silvey. They can thank your father that they're alive."

Iris refused to change her stand.

"It was a little early for Mullhall to be in town, wasn't it?" She put the loaded question with acid sweetness. "Unless he's been in all night, drunker than a Paiute, he never comes in from the ranch before noon. He got in for this little affair, didn't he?"

"You've got him all wrong for once," Jim argued.

He had more to say, and the more he insisted the more irked she became.

"You're getting to be as bad as Dad," she complained petulantly. "Let him get an idea into his head and it's impossible to reason with him.

42

With lawlessness running wild, will you tell me why neither one of you will admit for a moment that the most lawless man in the community may be responsible? I know Mullhall charges outrageous rates. But he pays no attention to his business, yet he's always rolling in money. Don't the two of you ever ask yourselves where it comes from?"

Jim grinned, thinking how truly she was a chip off the old block.

"We sure have," he said. "Bill's run out all his competition. If he never drew a sober breath from one week to the next, his reputation would keep the business going. The money he throws away is only loose change compared to what he's gouging out of the public."

"And I suppose his reputation explains why, with robberies being committed right and left, his stages are never held up." Iris's tone was frigidly sarcastic.

"I think that explains it. I'd say the fact that the stages are his is a pretty good guarantee that they'll go through unmolested. Road agents have a healthy respect for Bill Mullhall."

"You're taking a lot for granted, I think," Iris declared disparagingly. "I don't hear him threatening to sue the *Enterprise* for libel for what we've said about him. If I owned this sheet I'd go even further. I miss my guess if his ranch isn't a nest of thieves."

"That's going pretty far," Jim cautioned. "I've watched the place for days at a time. A tough bunch hangs out there, though I never saw anything to warrant what you're saying. You've always suspected the man and accused him of everything that's happened, but I never saw you get worked up like this. What's the reason for it?"

Iris hesitated for a moment. When she spoke her soberness pulled him up sharply.

"It's because I'm afraid—terribly afraid—for Dad. He's old, Jim—older than he realizes. He's always been able to take care of himself, no matter what came up. He thinks he can go on doing it forever. You know he can't, and so do I. When you told me how Bill Mullhall warned him this morning that dead sheriffs don't talk I felt my heart miss a beat. The man had something definite in mind, Jim. I can believe that part of it. Otherwise why would he have said it? Has Dad found some evidence against Mullhall?"

Jim pushed his chair back from the desk and gazed at her in reproving tight-lipped silence. "Now you listen to me, Iris, and get this straight," he said flatly. "You're worrying yourself needlessly. I grant you that Mullhall could give us the answers to a lot of things if he chose, but when he handed out that warning he wasn't warning Kize against himself; he was tipping him off against someone else."

He saw her cheeks blanch and realized too

late that he had unwittingly confirmed her fears.

"I thought I could smoke you out!" she cried. "Telling me I am worrying myself needlessly! Jim—who is it? Name him!"

"Please!" he protested with a vehemence not usually associated with him. "Do you think I'd be sitting here doing nothing if I knew? You've always agreed with your father and me that we're up against an organized gang. That may mean a dozen men or more. Chuck Silvey may be one of them. Chances are he is. But we can't be sure even about him; we're still in the dark. If things had worked out our way we'd have had a line on one or two of them today or tomorrow. No chance of it now."

Her keen sense of intuition was more than equal to the occasion.

"You mean Tom Yancey! You were counting on him to supply some information!"

Jim pulled down the corners of his mouth. "You'll have to supply your own answer to that," he muttered, getting to his feet. "I've said all I intend to say."

"Don't be cross with me, Jim," she begged. She caught his hand as she got up. "I'm beginning to understand what happened this morning. That outlaw gang knew Yancey had some evidence against Silvey, and he was ordered to kill the man before he could talk."

Jim shrugged and pretended not to be interested. "Your guess is as good as mine. But where would Bill Mullhall fit into that?"

Iris bit her lip. She had no answer ready, but it took her only a moment to find one.

"I can think of several explanations," said she. "By injecting himself into the affair he confused things in your mind and Dad's. Maybe that was his purpose. More likely he was there to make sure that Yancey hadn't had a chance to disclose his incriminating evidence before he was cut down. I haven't the slightest idea what that evidence amounted to, but I'm sure if there was a leak that threatened that cutthroat crowd with exposure because of some stupid move Chuck Silvey had made he would indeed have been shot down and his mouth closed as effectively as Yancey's was."

Though Jim Lord had a deep respect for her wisdom and insight and found the ideas she was expressing paralleling his own in some respects, he had no intention of admitting it and alarming her further. Instead he smiled and pretended not to be impressed.

"They're desperate men, Jim," she went on. "They wouldn't hesitate a moment about killing one of their own crowd to protect themselves. Don't treat what I'm saying as so much non-sense! It's true—horribly true! It's you and Dad I'm thinking about. They'll have even less compunction about killing you, once they see that you're closing in on them. You can't deny it, can you?"

"No," he acknowledged grudgingly. "There's very likely to be some gun smoke in this for us before we get to the end of it. But, as you've so often heard Kize say, that goes with the job. We're not rushing in blindfolded and taking unnecessary chances. I've told you again and again."

"I know," she murmured, trying to hold her voice steady, "but I'm getting so that I sit here afraid to look up when someone dashes in— afraid of the news they may be bringing me."

His arm went around her, and he drew her close for a moment.

"Keep your chin up, Iris; you're our anchor. We need you. I understand Hustis has been saying that it took the vigilantes to clean up Virginia City and Alder Gulch, and that's what we need here. I know he owns the paper. What he says privately won't cut much ice. But you see to it that the *Enterprise* doesn't start any campaign for a vigilance committee. It would be just the same as stabbing Kize in the back. You understand, don't you, Iris?"

"Of course. Promise me you'll stay close to him, Jim. I don't have to tell you to be careful for yourself. You know what you mean to me." She pulled his head down and kissed him.

When he released her, they discovered that

they were being spied on by a redheaded tot who had her freckled face pressed to the window. Her father was the *Enterprise*'s pressman. Iris waved to the child.

"Susie Galloway," she said with a wry smile. "I must be more careful in the future; I don't want to set Susie a bad example." Her dark mood was gone, and she appeared to be her usual cheerful self again. "Now you get out of here, Jim. I have a dozen things to do. Today's front page was about ready to be locked up. Now I'll have to go back and have the boys pull something and tell them to stand by for the Yancey story."

"Okay, lady, I'm as good as gone," he called out airily as he opened the door. He knew she had her feet on the ground once more, and he was immeasurably relieved.

Only the young woman who looked after the subscription list and the want ads was in the outer office. She had a smile for him as he passed. From the steps of the *Enterprise* office he glanced up and down the main street. Rock Creek appeared to have returned to its normal activity. On the sidewalk in front of the Maverick several men were gathered. One of them pointed to the spot where Tom Yancey had dropped. Obviously they were discussing the shooting. A few doors beyond the saloon a ranch wagon stood at the hitchrack. Halves of dressed beef were being carried into the Nevada Market, the town's leading butcher shop. Lord walked that way, definitely curious.

On approaching the wagon the two men who were handling the beef came out of the shop. He recognized them for two of Henry Dorn's ranch crew. He was about to speak to them when a man hailed him from the door of the market. It was Henry himself. He was one of the county commissioners, serving his fourth term, and generally regarded as the wealthiest stockman in the district.

"Mornin', Jim," said Henry. His greeting was not unfriendly, but it lacked its usual warmth. Lord had been one of Henry Dorn's Box D riders for three yeas and had had his support in getting his present appointment as paid deputy sheriff.

"Morning," Jim returned. "I figured you were too busy to be in town bossing the delivery of a wagonload of beef."

"I had to come in for the special meeting this afternoon. I just dropped into the market to collect some money that was owing. Another killing this morning. Right in town this time." He shook his head over the deplorable fact. "Things seem to be going from bad to worse."

"They're not getting any better," Jim conceded. "You commissioners are not helping matters by calling a special meeting and panning the sheriff. Our lawless element will sure get a bang out of that." He didn't propose to be put on the defensive, and with that in mind he changed the subject abruptly. "Have you got the hides for this beef?"

"Certainly!" Dorn drew himself up stiffly. "Damn it, man, you ain't questioning my honesty, be you?"

"We're not taking anything for granted, Henry; everybody gets treated alike. If you've got the hides, I want to see them."

"Well, I'll be damned!" Dorn snorted angrily. "Director of the bank, a county commissioner, running cattle on this range ever since it was Indian country, and you call me to account! Come with me! I'll show you the hides!"

He stormed into the Nevada Market and led the way to the back room.

"There's your hides!" he rapped. "You take a damned good look at 'em!"

"I'll be glad to," said Jim, not a bit intimidated by Henry's bluster.

He examined the brands carefully and counted the hides several times, making sure that the number tallied with the carcasses hanging on the rack. This was hardly necessary, but, figuratively speaking, he had the owner of the Box D on the hook, too, and he found a keen, though necessarily concealed, satisfaction in prolonging the man's agony.

"Everything seems to be in order," he announced finally, his tone as innocent as a babe's. "I'm sorry you've been annoyed, Henry. I can't understand your attitude; you know stock's being rustled, butchered, and the meat sold right here in town. If we check on everything that comes in we ought to be able to get a line on who's selling the rustled stuff. Didn't you vote for the ordinance making it mandatory for anyone with a dressed beef in his possession to produce the hide on demand?"

"I did!" Henry admitted hotly. "Nothing wrong with the principle of it if you use some sense in applying the law." Realizing that his bellowing had begun to attract attention out in front, he lowered his voice. He was no less indignant, however. "You and Kize know damn well I don't deal in rustled beef."

Jim shrugged with maddening equanimity. "Somebody's dealing in it, Henry—and no fly-by-night outfit either. If you want to do something helpful, tighten up the ordinance; make it impossible for the crooks to switch hides on us. I believe they're doing it. Forbid the sale of a beef carcass unless it has the hair on."

"That's impossible," Dorn declared promptly. "It wouldn't work; some of the eating-places couldn't use a whole beef at a time. The meat would spoil."

"Let them buy their stuff from the markets. It may cost them a penny or two a pound more, but they can afford it, with the prices they're getting for a meal. You can't set down to a steak in this town for less than six bits."

Jim glanced at his watch, though he was not particularly interested in the time of day. What he was really doing was trying to decide whether it would be worthwhile to give the commissioner another broadside. He told himself it couldn't do any harm.

"I'll have to be moving along," he said casually. "I'll see you this afternoon. I know what you'll have to say will be to the point. You're a fair man, Henry, and hardheaded, too; nobody ever found anything soft under your hat. I don't have to tell you that the board won't be fooling anyone, not even itself, if it tries to pass the buck and shove all the responsibility for present conditions on Kize. The board's got to shoulder some of it and back him up. You'll hear from the public if you don't. Of course that doesn't apply to you, Henry; you can be re-elected as often as you want to run. But some of the other members didn't have any votes to spare last election. You might remind 'em of that."

Chapter Four

A PRICELESS STORY

Jim sailed out of the Nevada Market without waiting for Dorn to give him an answer.

I don't know whether I lit a fire under him or not, he mused as he went up the street. *I wouldn't mind too much if that bunch asked me to turn in my badge, but I don't want them to pull Kize down.*

The board was composed of four members, three of them stockmen and the fourth, Amos Hardesty, the president of Rock Creek's only bank. Hardesty usually sided with Dorn. He chanced to step out of the bank as Jim was passing. They spoke briefly.

"Another unfortunate incident this morning," the banker observed. He was a stoop-shouldered harried-looking man whose health had been failing for years. "I was glad to hear that Kize made Bill Mullhall back down. That's something to commend, at least."

"I wouldn't say he made him back down, Mr. Hardesty," Jim returned. "But he stood up to him and told him where he headed in. I haven't seen anybody else stand up to him. Perhaps that's because I don't get around as much as some of you county commissioners. Maybe you've seen someone that I missed."

Hardesty got the dig and made a long face.

"Possibly," he said in a sepulchral voice. "I, for one, have never asked the impossible of Kize. I know these are trying times. The public has been very patient with the sheriff. Very!"

With a curt good morning he continued on his way.

Old Moneybags would like to lift Kize's scalp if he had the nerve, thought Jim. *Stick a knife into him and I'll bet you'd get ice water!*

Not too many years back the bank had been in the process of being held up. Kize had foiled the robbery and saved the day for Amos Hardesty. Some things were quickly forgotten, Jim told himself.

He glanced through windows as he went by the hotel. Some of the regulars who spent most of their time in the lobby were on hand. He failed to catch sight of Con Morgan or Chuck Silvey.

Cutting diagonally across the street at the courthouse corner, he was hailed by a horseman who pulled his bronc to a slithering stop.

"Hi, Jim!" the grinning rider yelped. He was a freckled red-haired man with a pair of baby-blue eyes set in a face that was both humorous and reckless.

"Hi, Oats!" Lord returned. Here was an old

friend, and he was glad to see him. "How's everything on Cabin Creek?"

"Couldn't be better! Cows eatin' and drinkin' and begettin'! Say, has Kize done anythin' about me yet?"

"It's coming up this afternoon, Oats. He's putting it up to the commissioners. You going to be around town the rest of the day?"

"Yeh. The boss sent me in for some things."

"Fine," said Jim. "Be on your good behavior. No elbow-bending, understand?"

"Shore! I want that job, Jim."

"You drop around to the office and see Kize after the meeting," he was advised.

Kize had his feet on his desk and was tipped far back in his chair, still meditating on the events of the morning when Jim walked in.

"You got things figured out?" Jim inquired.

"Jest about." Kize took down his feet and straightened up. "Where you been?"

"I ran into Dorn and needled him up a bit."

Kize forgot his cares long enough to chuckle over what Jim had to say.

"When he was listin' his accomplishments didn't that psalm-singin' Baptist say anythin' about bein' a deacon of the church?" Kize queried.

"No, he was too mad."

The old man laughed. "Hank Dorn's all right. I've got worse friends. If he supports me, I don't care what the other members of the board have to say. Hank can back 'em into a fence corner if he gits his dander up. You seen Iris?"

"Yes. She called me in for a few minutes."

Kize gave him a sharp glance. "What'd you tell her?"

"Nothing that she couldn't have got from someone else. Funny, her slant on Con. She thinks Silvey's got something on Morgan."

"Does she?" Kize picked up his tobacco pouch. "I'm wonderin' about that myself," he muttered as he filled his pipe. Without warning he popped a question at Lord. "What's your slant?"

"There's something between them. Wild Bill knows what it is. Struck me they were almost as afraid of what he might say as they were of his guns. Either Silvey and his pals have turned up something and are putting the screws on Morgan or—and I don't like to say this—it's the other way around, and he's giving the orders to them."

The sheriff puffed his pipe gravely and was slow to answer. "I wonder," he mused aloud. "Comes hard to suspect a man you've had faith in for years. Con's got brains. Chuck Silvey is just a low-grade crook; he couldn't be headman of anythin'. We better go slow and not leap to any conclusions. Mebbe they've jest got together on the gamblin' business. That could be the deal."

Jim shook his head. "You don't believe that, Kize. You know it's bigger than that. Tom Yancey had nothing to do with the gambling racket."

Kize nodded grimly. "That's true. We think we know why he was bumped off, but we can't be shore."

"We can be sure of some other things," Lord persisted. "Con Morgan has owned the Bar 66 spread for two or three years. He uses a lot of beef. I don't know whether that explains anything or not, but it's worth looking into."

"It is," the old man agreed. He got up and began pacing the floor of the little room, hands clasped behind his back. "My ace didn't stand up, but we've been dealt some cards. Mebbe some high cards. We'll see—we'll see. Otis was in here a bit ago all hot and bothered. I'm afraid I wasn't much help to him. I referred him to Cap. I think we'll be better off if we let this killin' go down as self-defense. We'll always have time to change our mind. You can't catch big fish, Jim, if yo're satisfied to go after minnows."

Their discussion had dragged on for half an hour or more when the door opened suddenly and a colorless little man popped in and immediately closed the door behind him.

His rough garb and heavy boots identified him as one of the small army of miners working the gravel in Rustlers' Bend. Furthermore, Kize and Jim recognized him as one of the several men in from the diggings they had seen in the Maverick that morning.

The visitor appeared nervous, even frightened. Since he had not passed the window, which he would have had to do had he reached the office by coming up the sidewalk from the main street, they knew he had arrived by way of the back lots.

"Wal," Kize questioned, "what can I do for you?"

"My name is Ike Burch," the stranger answered, shying away from the window. "I want to talk to you, sheriff, and I don't want no one to see me in here. If that bunch finds out that I been confabin' with you I'll git the same dose they handed Tom. You got some place where we can talk private?"

"There's jest this office and the cells in the rear," Kize told him. This man Burch had said enough already to arouse the keenest sort of interest and speculation in the sheriff and Jim. "There's a passageway leads through that door to the cell block. If anyone comes you can step in there till they're gone."

Burch indicated the outer door with a jerk of his head. "You mind lockin' it?"

"Hell's fire, we ain't had a key for it in years. Jim, pull yore chair up in front of the door and sit there. You take this seat alongside my desk, mister, and let's hear what you got to say."

"Tom Yancey and me was friends, and long before we saw Rustlers' Bend," Burch began. "I bumped into him by accident this mornin'. He told me what he was doin' in town. It was the first

I'd heard about him seein' a couple of fellas leave the Bend that mornin' with Jeff Foraker. Tom said he'd promised you he'd try to spot at least one of those gents, and he was goin' to make the rounds of the saloons in the hopes of locatin' him. You follow me?"

"Good gravy, yes!" Kize snapped. "Keep on talkin'!"

"Tom was a mite nervous; he figgered it might have got back to certain parties that he'd been seen talkin' to you. He asked me if I'd mind taggin' along after him. He was to go into a bar first, and I was to stroll in a few seconds later. I wasn't to mix up in any trouble he might walk into nor even let on I knew him. What he wanted to be sure of was that if he recognized one of the those birds he could tip me off and I could git word back to you, no matter what happened to him. Wal, that's the way we worked it. We'd been in and out of four, five places before we walked into the Maverick. When Tom came face to face with Chuck Silvey he pushed his hat back on his head. That was the signal that he'd found his man. What—"

"Hold up a minute!" Kize interrupted. His old eyes were pin points of excitement. "You shore you got the signal straight?"

"Course I'm sure!" Burch declared. "Tom turned to me after he gave it to make sure I'd got it. I nodded that I had."

Kize Farraday was hard put to contain himself. He slapped his weather-beaten hat on the desk, and his smothered whoop of satisfaction almost choked him. "We're gittin' a break at last!" he crowed. "And what a break, Jim! So Silvey was one of the pair that knocked off Jeff Foraker!" He rubbed his hands together in unholy glee, looking more like a fierce, implacable old eagle than ever. "Ike, you don't know what this means to us. I swear to you Tom Yancey will be avenged, and many times over before we're through. Did Tom draw on him?"

"He didn't have a chance to draw. Them wolves was waitin' for him. When his drink came Silvey upset it and shot him down before you could say Jack Robinson. Tom staggered back. He was halfway to the door before he got his gun out of the holster. He tried to get it up, but he was too far gone to do anythin'. It happened so quick I wouldn't have seen it if I hadn't been lookin' for something like that."

"Where was Con Morgan?" Jim spoke up.

"He was there alongside Silvey. He purtended to be awful shocked. But he didn't fool me; he knew it was comin'."

"You're stating an opinion now," Jim remarked. "What you thought about it won't be admitted as evidence. Did you see Morgan do or hear him say anything that indicated he was a party to what happened?"

Burch thought it over for a moment or two. "No," he admitted, "I don't know as I did. I reckon it's what he didn't do that damns him. When a man whips out a gun beside you you jump back and try to git out of the way. Morgan never moved a finger. He didn't even look surprised."

"That's evidence," Kize said. "It ain't conclusive, but it's admissible. Morgan may be able to explain it. But let's go back to the beginnin'. Did Yancey say anythin' to you about Bill Mullhall?"

"Not this mornin'. But he knew Wild Bill. Mullhall may be a diamondback rattler with some, but he didn't have a finger in this frame-up."

Though Ike Burch's story was priceless beyond words and Kize had little reason to doubt it was true, he was not satisfied; he had to be sure. With that in mind he led the man over it, back and forth half a dozen times, deliberately trying to confuse him and break it down. Try as he would —and he had Jim's help—he could neither develop any discrepancies nor catch Burch in any contradic-tions.

"That settles it," he declared at last. "You know what yo're talkin' about. I want you to go back to the Bend and keep away from me till I need you."

"Oh, no!" Burch demurred. "I ain't goin' back

to the Bend! I sold my claim an hour ago to Mike Brophy; I ain't even goin' up to git my tools and my tent. I'm gittin' outa this country. If you want to call in a shorthand writer I'll make a statement and sign it, but I ain't stickin' around here to git bumped off."

Jim expected the old man to voice instant objection to such a program. Instead Kize said, "There's somethin' to that. The only shore way I could protect you would be to lock you up, and that would be good only so long. Where you aimin' to head for?"

"Reno. I'll give you an address where you can keep in touch with me. I'll come back when you can guarantee me it'll be safe. It's less than three hours till the afternoon train pulls out for the south. I'll ask you to look out for me till she goes."

"We'll do that," Kize agreed. "Jim, you take down his statement in longhand. When you git done go around to the barn and hitch the bays to a buggy. Bring some sandwiches back with you—enough for the two of you. I'm goin' to have you drive Ike down to McCardlesville. He can catch the train there. You stick close to him till the train's movin'."

"I'll do that," Lord agreed. "I won't be back in time for the meeting."

"Forgit about the meetin'," Kize grumbled. "Trade seats with me and git busy; I'll take care of Hank Dorn and the rest of them politicians!"

Chapter Five

ATTACK BY A BULLY

The afternoon was gone by the time Deputy Sheriff Lord got back to Rock Creek. The southbound train had not left town until an hour after its scheduled departure, emergency repairs on the locomotive—a leaking steam chest, this time, which had to be repacked—the reason. It was not an unusual circumstance for the N. and I., for its antiquated rolling stock, ready for the junk pile when the little railroad purchased it from the defunct Iowa Central, was always breaking down. He had put Ike Burch safely aboard the train at McCardlesville and begun the long drive back north at once.

While Jim returned to town anxious to learn how Kize had fared with the county commissioners, he had another matter on his mind of equal importance. Though he understood the old man's motive in helping Burch to flee the country and was in full accord with it, he could not blink the fact that Kize had again grossly exceeded his authority and left himself open to the serious charge of having secreted a witness to a felony.

It went without saying that Jim found himself

in the same boat. He was determined to have it out with Kize at once; if Burch disappeared, as key witnesses had a habit of doing, the two of them could be charged with malfeasance in office and caught without any hope of defending themselves.

The afternoon had turned unseasonably warm. After putting up the team Jim came up the path from the barn to find Kize sitting out in front of the office thoughtfully puffing on his pipe, his short legs crossed. It was enough to tell him that the old man had not fared too badly at the hands of the commissioners.

Kize brought his chair down on all fours and unwound his legs on catching sight of him. "Back, eh?" he said. "I heard the train pulled out late; I knew you wouldn't be back much before evenin'. You git him off all right?"

Jim nodded. "No trouble at all. Coming up the path I noticed you grinning to yourself like an old tomcat. How'd the meeting go?"

Kize chuckled immodestly. "It went my way. Before they got through with me I wangled money for another paid depity out of 'em and got an emergency ordinance makin' it unlawful to offer a beef for sale if the hide's been pulled. Wrangled with 'em for two hours. They was all set to throw the book at me and Otis. I'm danged if the boy didn't surprise me, the way he made them back water."

Jim reached in through the open door and got a chair.

"What do you mean?" he asked with a puzzled frown.

"Why, Woodhull had no sooner called the meetin' to order than he and George Rainey, the penny-pinchin' ignoramus, began yappin' about no convictions, no arrests, the country goin' to hell in general. I figgered I better save my ammunition and let Otis take first crack at 'em. So help me, he stood up and told them he wasn't there to be cross-examined—that there'd be arrests when he was convinced they could be followed up with convictions. The ringleaders of the outlaw element was the ones he was after, he said. He had information in his possession that was so startlin' and incriminating that he didn't feel free to divulge it even to them. And he swung around and warned me not to say a word, lest there be a leak and all our work go for nothin'.''

"Good heavens, Kize, has he really got hold of something?" Jim questioned incredulously.

"No, of course not! But they swallowed it; they wasn't prepared for any stand like that from Otis. I reckon that's why it went down so easy. All he's got to do now is make his bluff good. And we got to help him, Jim; I forgave Otis a lot this after-noon."

Kize spoke freely of his brush with the commissioners.

"The fireworks started poppin' when I demanded another depity," he continued. "Rainey and Hardesty hit the ceilin'; they wasn't standin' for such reckless extravagance, they said. Accordin' to them, me and you had handled things satisfactorily in the past and there wasn't no reason why we couldn't do it now if we put our minds to it. I just had to hammer it into their heads that things is a bit different, with a couple thousand wild-eyed miners and stampeders to ride herd on. Hank Dorn took up the fight for me and talked 'em down." Kize shook his head disgustedly. "It began all over again when I told 'em I wanted to swear in Oats Ollinger. Hardesty threw up his hands in horror and told me I was crazy—that Oats would have all of us in hot water before he was on the job twenty-four hours. Called him a wild, reckless, fightin' fool who'd been huntin' trouble ever since he was old enough to put on overalls. By gravy, I told him that a fightin' fool was exactly what I wanted! Oats has gone out to the ranch; he'll be in tomorrow mornin' to take the oath."

The news pleased Jim. "Oats will come through for us. His laugh and grin fool a lot of people, but when the chips are down he's got what it takes. We can't have any secrets from him, Kize; we'll have to give it to him straight about Yancey and Burch and all the rest of it."

"Naturally," the old man agreed.

"What about Burch?" Jim demanded, a new note of soberness in his voice. "You know you've left yourself wide open for trouble in not taking him before the D.A."

"I shore have," was Kize's gruff response. "If I had let him tell his story to Otis, Silvey would have been charged with murder and I would have been ordered to take him into custody. The best we could have got out of that would have been to have him found guilty. By grab, I'm playin' for bigger stakes than that. I figger by keepin' our mouths shut and just sawin' wood we may be able to snag bigger game than him. The gamble's worth the risk. You can't lick this proposition by trimmin' its edges; you've got to smash through to the heart of it. You remember that, Jim, if anythin' happens to me."

He mentioned this somber possibility with a characteristic absence of concern for himself. Lord attempted to treat it lightly.

"Nothing's going to happen to you," he said.

Kize grunted skeptically. "Don't let us kid ourselves, Jim; no man's luck stands up forever. That goes for you as well as for me, and it'll go for Oats, too. You ain't seen the *Enterprise* yet?"

"No. How did Iris handle the story?"

"She didn't play it up too much. Quotes me and Otis and Cap Wyeth as agreeing that Yancey was at fault and Silvey was justified in shootin'. It's awful hard to fool Iris. I couldn't come right out and tip her off, but I dropped a hint or two, and I reckon she smelled a rat. Leastwise she didn't write anythin' that she'll have to eat one of these days. There's a copy of the *Enterprise* on the desk if you want to have a look at it."

Jim stepped inside and was reading the paper when the marshal came up the walk and took his vacated chair. Jim could hear him talking.

"I'll relieve yuh of the two boys yuh got in the cooler," Cap announced. "Somebody appeared before Judge Messenger and paid their fine, and he signed an order for their release."

The town had no lockup of its own and used the county jail. The two prisoners, cowboys who had been arrested as the result of a street fight, had been brought in by Cap.

Kize walked back with him and let the two men out of their cells. Though the latter still bore marks of their melee, they came out laughing, their enmity buried, and bore no one any ill will. They passed Lord on their way to the street. They joshed with him for a moment.

"See you again," was Jim's jocular farewell.

"No, you won't!" one of them called back. "We don't like the grub you serve up here, and there ain't enough of it."

Kize and Cap walked into the office together.

"Hear they give yuh another paid depity," Cap remarked. "Wonder when them tightwads will git around to givin' me a man or two."

"I don't know; I'm no fortune teller," Kize told him.

"Hunh!" Cap snorted indignantly. "I didn't expect any sympathy from yuh! Nobody appreciates what I do." He grumbled to himself as he went out.

Kize was ready to leave a few minutes later.

"Iris will have supper waitin'," he said. "You goin' to be around this evenin'?"

"I'll be around," said Jim.

"All right. We'll sit down and try to map out somethin'. We're goin' to keep cases on Chuck Silvey and the bunch he travels with. And I'm including Con. We'll ride up to the Bend tomorrow and make a little scout over to the east afterward and give his spread a good lookin' over."

The night passed without incident. At different times both Kize and Jim looked in at the hotel and the Maverick bar. Con was very much present, but nothing was to be seen of Chuck Silvey.

When they came down next morning they found Oats on hand. He had brought his own string of broncs with him. In the few minutes he had been around he had already made himself at home. With his presence the drab old office became a merrier place. He believed that everything had a bright side, and he managed to find it.

Kize swore him in and set him to swabbing out the cells, a task that seldom had any attention.

"That'll take him down a peg," the old man confided to Jim. "I'll find ways to cool him off a bit before he's been around here very long."

It was after ten when they pulled out of town for Rustlers' Bend. On the way Kize took his new deputy into his confidence and told him exactly how matters stood. It had a surprisingly sobering effect on Oats. He was particularly impressed with Jim's thought that Con Morgan's Bar 66 ranch might be involved in the rustling. The Cabin Creek Livestock Company, for whom Oats had been riding, had range in the Buckskin foothills adjacent to Bar 66. Along with the rest of his old crew he had indulged in the usual bunkhouse gossip regarding neighboring ranches.

"You may have hit the nail on the head," he declared. "That would explain a thing or two, at least."

"How?" Kize asked.

"He's got a new crew and a new man ramrodin' the spread. He lost three of the old bunch almost as soon as the excitement began. They got gold fever. Since then he's replaced the others one at a time. The only one of 'em who ever worked on this range before is Steve Gore, and his reputation was never too good. We just couldn't savvy why Con was turnin' off good men and hirin' on strangers. He turned Honey Ricker adrift. Honey's a top hand. He caught on with our outfit right away. He told us he'd never had any trouble with Con and couldn't understand why he'd been handed his time."

Jim caught the old man's eye. "It makes me wonder more than ever if we haven't put our finger on something."

"Yeh," Kize muttered thoughtfully. "I knew Con had hired a new foreman and two or three punchers. I didn't know all of the old crew was gone. We'll shore look into it."

They were still several miles from the Bend when one of Wild Bill's stages bore down on them, the six-horse team on the dead run kicking up clouds of dust, and the heavy coach heaving and lurching precariously on its leather thorough braces as it plunged in and out of the treacherous chuckholes with which the road was pitted.

"They're in one hell of a hurry," Oats commented. Mullhall's stages usually moved more sedately.

The sheriff and his deputies drew off to the side of the road, and as the careening stage swept past them they were surprised to see Wild Bill on the box with the driver. They raised a hand in the customary greeting. Bill saw them, but he did not respond. In their brief glimpse of him they realized from the set of his jaw and flaming eyes that he was in one of his uglier moods.

"Wonder what he's got on his mind this mornin'," Kize growled. "If I know him, he's had a run-in with somebody."

The explanation was waiting for them when they reached the tiny settlement that had grown up around the dilapidated, weather-beaten frame building that Johnnie Montero had built in the long ago to house his back-country saloon. In those days Juan Montero—everybody called him Johnnie—and his customers had had Rustlers' Bend to themselves. Rock Creek could be forded in many places, but the crossing where he established himself had soon become the main thoroughfare to the north and east. Locally it was most often spoken of as Spanish Ford.

There were Basque sheepmen in the Buckskins where the graze was too poor to support cattle. Being a Basque, Johnnie catered to his country-men. Cowboys resorted there, too. They had no personal quarrel with the Basques, but the ancient partisan feud of cowman and herder lay between them and resulted in periodic brawling. A third gentry, a hard-faced crew who did their riding by night, sometimes rendezvoused there. They were free spenders.

Johnnie asked them no questions and never had any information concerning them to relay to the sheriff. He was a profane, laughing, barrel-chested man with the strength of an ox. The discovery of gold had appeared to be his great opportunity; day and night a wild gold-crazed mob crowded into his bar, the only one in camp, threatening to tear the place apart. Armed with a stout pickax handle, he tried to maintain a semblance of order. It was a losing battle. When his establishment had been wrecked for the fifth time he acknowledged defeat and turned the place into a general store. He still dispensed whisky, but it had to be purchased by the bottle or gallon and could not be consumed on the premises.

Montero's place was flanked right and left by half a dozen board-and-canvas places of business, some boasting false Cripple Creek fronts. Across the way a score of tents housed an unknown number of female camp followers who brazenly plied what has so often been termed the oldest profession in the world.

Recently the post office in Rock Creek had established a branch office at the Bend. It was housed in a corner of Johnnie's store, with Little Ben Riley in charge. Little Ben had proved himself a popular character. He was an inoffensive man, crippled with a withered right foot. No one envied him his job; it paid very little. To eke out a living Little Ben helped Johnnie in the store in his spare time.

This morning with his first glimpse of Spanish Ford and the sprouting settlement Kize saw at least a score of men milling around in front of Montero's store. They were men from the adjacent diggings and normally should have been at work at this hour.

"The mail came up long ago," Kize remarked, immediately concerned. "That ain't what they're waitin' around for. Come on!"

He spurred his bronc, and Jim and Oats quickened their pace. Several minutes later they pulled up at the store. There was a wide platform or stoop several steps off the ground in front of Montero's place. Leaving his horse at the rack, the sheriff hurried across the platform and into the store. Johnnie was in the rear with several men. One of them was Chuck Silvey.

"What's this all about?" Kize asked when he had called the Basque aside.

"Wild Bill Mullhall!" Johnnie used both his native Spanish and inadequate English profanity to express his opinion of that individual. That attended to, he said, "He ees come theece morning and tell us we're pay four bits a hondred more for evert'ing he haul up from town. Las' week she ees four bits more. Every week he raise his rate, the goddam hog! What he t'ink we are? Pay heem more for haul sack of flour up from Rock Creek than flour ees worth?"

"Go on," Kize urged. "Tell me what happened."

"Plentay men in for the mail. They hear what he say. By Joe, they not like theece beezness, pay through the nose for everyt'ing, and they tell him so. Wild Bill, he don't geeve damn for not'ing like that; he laugh in their face and tell 'em to get out. Everybody afraid of him but Little Ben. Ees meestake for him to say anyt'ing, but he have to shoot hees mouth off. He say some fella is all ready to settle Bill's hash. I don' know where he get that—just bluff, I tank. But Bill, he go crazy and slam hell out of him. He knock him down, pick him up, knock him down. By damn, that make me mad—beeg fella like Mullhall beat up crip'!" Just talking about it made Johnnie's wrath boil over. "I make sure I stop eet, I tank! I run to back of store and get my club. Don't take long, but Mullhall has Little Ben by the collar and drag him outside. He kick him down the step. *Ese hombre es una fiera*! Goddam, I tank I keel Wild Bill. The stage is stand there ready to leave, the guards up on roof. One of them, Frank Woodmancy, see me run out. He pick up his shotgun and tell me he blow my head off if I move. *Virgen santisima*! That stop me! Wild Bill tell us all to go to hell, and he climb up on the box with the driver, and off they go."

Questions were leaping into Kize's mind, and they were in no way concerned with the brutality of Mullhall's attack on Little Ben Riley; the whole incident needed explaining, and he could not escape the feeling that factors were involved that did not appear on the surface.

"Does Riley need a doctor, Johnnie?"

Montero shook his head. "Chuck got him patch up; he be all right."

"Good," Kize muttered. "I'm surprised that

75

Silvey didn't take a hand in the scrap when he saw his friend Riley gittin' a beatin'. Chuck was in the store, I reckon, while all this was goin' on."

"No, it was all over when he came in." Johnnie lowered his voice against being overheard at the rear of the store. "Ees damn fool, Chuck; show up here last night after what happen in town. Tom Yancey have plentay friend along the Bend."

"No charges against Silvey," Kize observed without interest. "He must have had some business to attend to."

"Beezness? Blond beezness, you mean." Montero winked an eye and chuckled knowingly. "When he see how the boys feel he don't stick around long last night; he talk to Little Ben, and then he go across the street. He don't show his face again till a few minutes ago. I just tell him if he got any sense he get out of camp."

Kize had found the fishing excellent. With Montero he walked back for a word with Little Ben, who was stretched out on an unused counter, his face patched up with court plaster, his mouth badly swollen.

Silvey had an impersonal nod of recognition for the old man; Riley looked up at him with his shrewd beetlelike eyes.

"Johnnie's just been tellin' me that Bill gave you a good beatin'," said Kize. "Looks like he wasn't lyin'. Why did you put yore oar in, Ben?

You don't have no freight comin' up from town."

"The principle of the thing got me. I'm sick of seeing that dirty stinker putting his hand in everybody's pocket. He can lick me with one hand tied behind his back, but I showed him I wasn't afraid to tell him off to his teeth."

Kize found it an entirely unbelievable explanation, but he pretended not to question it. "You knew what you was askin' for," said he. "You ought to be satisfied; you got it. You filin' any charges against Bill Mullhall?"

"No, I'll get satisfaction some other way." Little Ben's eyes burned a little brighter. "He's about to the end of his rope. Folks stand for just so much from a skunk like him; then one day they decide they've had enough, and they do something about it. I won't have to wait long. Mullhall went too far when he kicked a cripple around."

Kize was immediately convinced that there was no longer any mystery about Little Ben's purpose in inviting a beating at Wild Bill's hands. Fitting Chuck Silvey into the picture did not tax his imagination. Poker-faced, he said, "Could be. No doubt there's certain parties would be well pleased to see Wild Bill run out of the country. But don't underestimate the man, Ben, or you'll wish you'd climbed into one of your mailbags and thrown away the key."

Big Johnnie Montero held his sides and roared with laughter. "By Joe, that's good! You get in one of them mailbag, Ben, and Uncle Sam say, 'Hands off,' eh?"

Silvey found nothing amusing about it. "If three or four hundred men get organized they'll take things over."

"It won't take that many," said Kize. "If it happens, Wild Bill won't be the only one they'll go after; there'll be other names on their list. I'd keep that in mind. In fact I'd do some thinkin' about it right now; that crowd out in front seems to be growin'. Mebbe they're jest discussin' the weather; mebbe they're not. Tom Yancey ain't been laid in his grave yet."

The sheriff had had his say. He swung around and left them standing there. Jim Lord came across the platform to join him at the door. A few yards away the crowd, numbering over thirty now, regarded them with sullen disapproval.

"I understand Silvey's horse is in Johnnie's barn," said Jim. "He better climb aboard and get out of here. These men aren't fooling, Kize; they want him. They're just waiting till we pull away."

"Wal, if that's the case, we'll stick around a bit," the old man growled. "Silvey's had all the warnin' he's goin' to git from me. Too dang bad we can't afford to let these fellas go to work on him. Tell Oats to git down; we may be here some time."

Selecting an empty wooden box from a pile, at the side of the platform, he placed it on end and sat down. As further proof that he was not leaving he produced pipe and tobacco.

The crowd perceived his intention at once. An angry muttering arose from the men. Two or three minutes later, however, their attention was diverted by the appearance of a mounted man who swung out wide around the wood-and-canvas shack that housed a blacksmith's forge and headed for the crossing. It was Chuck Silvey. The crowd ran that way, hooting and yelling. Several shots were fired that went hopelessly wide of the mark. Silvey pulled his bronc to a gallop and dashed across the creek to disappear in the hills beyond.

"That yellowleg was sure makin' tracks!" Oats observed thinly. "Where's he lightin' out for in that direction?"

"Con Morgan's Bar 66, if you're asking me," said Jim.

"Git mounted!" Kize rapped. "We're headin' that way, too!"

Chapter Six

MIDNIGHT STAMPEDE

In carving its present course Rock Creek had cut deeply into the Buckskin Hills so that in most places the outer curve of Rustlers' Bend was a sheer bank rising thirty to forty feet above the creek bottom. Vegetation had long ago caught a foothold there and even in dry years had continued to flourish, and the creek bottom was green with aspens, some pine, the ubiquitous cottonwood, and great patches of glossy mountain mahogany.

On the lower, or inside, curve gold had been discovered. It was a gentle bank, sloping gradually upward to a mountain meadow. Kize Farraday had often called it the "purtiest stretch of country this side of heaven" in the days before the rush began. Now it was dotted with a crazy quilt of tents and brush wickiups built in the Paiute fashion, and pock-marked with countless scars of shovel and pick. To the north its beauty remained unspoiled, the creek breaking through a towering rocky portal to pour its precious waters into the Bend.

No matter what haste he was in, Kize always had a moment to contemplate the rugged grandeur of that exciting panorama. Today was no exception. He tried not to see the hideous changes man had wrought—the gashed earth, the water muddied with the gravel of the sluice boxes, the denuded bars that had been burned off to make the placering easier, and the endless litter that strews every landscape where men are intent only on ripping out a fortune in a hurry. But he couldn't close his eyes to them; they were there, and they made him wince.

"It's a massacre!" he muttered bitterly to himself. "When that mob gits through with the Bend there won't be nothin' left. Not even the Paiutes will want it!"

Jim dropped back and rode beside him.

"You talking to yourself?" he asked.

"Jest thinkin' out loud," was Kize's crusty answer. "We'll pull up when we get to the top of the ridge. If Silvey's goin' to Bar 66 we'll be able to spot him."

When they reached the crest a vast expanse of territory lay spread out before them. This ridge was the divide between Rock Creek and the headwaters of Cabin Creek. To their right the broken hills flattened out to pleasant, rolling rangeland.

"There he goes, cuttin' across to the south fork of the crick!" Oats called out. "He's behind that long patch of mahogany now. Watch the lower end; you'll see him directly."

It wasn't long before Silvey reappeared, jogging along without any thought of pursuit.

"He's bound for Bar 66 jest as Jim said," Kize declared. "We won't chase him; we'll drift through the hills this afternoon on the chance that we may git a line on somethin' and drop down Morgan's way toward evenin'. Git out yore glasses, Jim, and have a look at the country. See if you can find a trace of smoke anywheres. Rustlin's been reported from way over on Wildcat and Seven Springs. If Bar 66 is where the stuff's been going they've had to hold it somewheres. You can't drive stock that distance between sunset and sunup."

Lord used his binoculars for ten minutes and failed to find any sign of smoke or horsemen. Under the bright midday sun the Buckskin Hills appeared to slumber peacefully. High up on the flank of Fremont Peak a band of Angel Begoa's sheep moved into view, but that did not come within their interest.

"We'll git off the ridge and work across toward Seven Springs," said Kize. "We wanted to have a look around there the last time we was out, Jim. This will be a good time to do it."

He hadn't said a word about what had taken place at Spanish Ford. Jim had thought to wait him out. Wearying of that, he brought it up himself.

"I thought you boys had figgered that play out,"

Kize told him. "No mystery about it. Little Ben is a cute customer. He crossed Wild Bill deliberately. I don't know as he counted on gittin' the beatin' Bill gave him, but, whether he expected it or not, it made his play stand up. There's been a lot of feelin' against Bill. This may snowball into somethin' serious. At least, that was the idea."

This was a riddle to Oats. "I don't get it. I never heard of Mullhall makin' any trouble for Little Ben."

"Put the pieces together and you'll have the answer," the old man said bluntly. "Chuck Silvey's no fool; he knew he was likely to run into trouble at the crossin'. So he came for a reason. I figger it was to give Riley some instructions. The two of 'em had their heads together last night; what happened this mornin' was planned."

Oats looked his surprise. "You mean Little Ben's workin' under cover for somebody?"

"We've thought so for a long while," Jim informed him. "We've watched him, but he's been too slick for us. I'd say that this only goes to prove we've been right about him all along. We've been just following hunches and stabbing in the dark, but the whole thing is beginning to jell in my mind."

"Mine, too," Kize seconded. "Little Ben Riley is the chief informer for the gang of crooks we're after. He's in a position to know who's leavin' camp and when. A man can keep his mouth shut if he's pullin' away with a sizable amount of gold on him, but he's always shore to go to Riley and leave a forwardin' address for his mail. If two or three men band together for safety's sake and go out by wagon he finds some way of putting a mark on it that the gang can read. That's the only way I can explain what happened to the bunch that was drivin' across the mountains to Idaho. They didn't git far before they was stuck up. One of 'em lived long enough to tell me that Little Ben was the only person who knew they was leavin' and which way they was travelin'."

Oats was quick to grasp the meaning of all this and equally quick to realize that it was more surmise than provable fact. Kize and Jim could only agree with him.

"But what's the angle on Mullhall?" he asked.

"They're afraid of him," said Jim. "You'd have got it if you'd been in the Maverick yesterday morning. Bill can name names and say who's who. He's got a tough bunch working for him, some of them with records of their own. They can spot a crook when they bump into one. It didn't take him long to add up the score. That's enough in itself to make him dangerous. But I don't believe that's the only reason why they're out to get Bill Mullhall."

"Nor me," old Kize agreed. "They're most likely afraid he's goin' to horn in on their game or take it over complete. They'd like nothin' better than to see a mob string him up."

They began moving down the slope, with Oats leading the way. He turned in his saddle to ask where Johnnie Montero stood.

"You don't have to worry about Johnnie," Kize assured him. "He's sorta taken Little Ben under his wing, but that's on the up-and-up, as far as he's concerned. He ain't mixed up in this deal."

The afternoon was half gone before they were in position to scour the badlands north and west of Seven Springs. It was broken country, crisscrossed by mean little canyons, more than one of which would have served admirably to hold a hidden corral. This unfenced range was part of John Woodhull's thirty-thousand-acre spread. The graze was so poor, however, that his Double Diamond cattle seldom got this far north.

No rain had fallen here since late spring. The earth was powder-dry, and such tracks of horses and cows as they found were drifted over and almost obliterated.

Kize held up his hand and called a halt.

"Looks like we're wastin' our time," he admitted reluctantly. "If any stuff had been driven through here recently we'd have seen some sign of it by now. The two of you got anythin' to suggest?"

"I don't know," Jim said, lowering his binoculars after another fruitless searching of the country ahead of them. "We could play our hunch all the way out. I don't know that it'll stand up, but if we knew for a fact that the rustled stuff is being hazed through to Bar 66 we wouldn't be looking around here for a hidden corral. If you cut out a bunch of cows around Seven Springs or along Wildcat and wanted to get them through unseen to Morgan's spread you'd most likely take to the desert and cut back by way of the Red Buttes or Touchstone Canyon. Least that'd be my way of doing it."

Kize greeted it with a noncommittal grunt. But he clamped his lips together tightly and screwed up his eyes in a brooding squint which was characteristic of him when he was turning over any matter of weighty concern in his mind.

Oats Ollinger scratched his head and pointed out what to him was a flaw in Jim's reasoning. "Anybody drivin' in from the Buttes or through Touchstone would have to cross Cabin Crick sooner or later if they wanted to git west to Morgan's place. You know without my tellin' you that there's ranches along the crick. Not all but most of that range is fenced off. Chances are you'd have trouble gettin' through with a bunch of cows."

"I don't know why," Kize spoke up. "There ain't been no stock run off down that way; nobody's out lookin' for rustlers. Where nobody's lookin' for you is the place to git through. We'll move along to Hank Dorn's and invite ourselves to supper. Afterward we'll take a chance on Touchstone. We can be in the canyon by ten o'clock. We'll lay out there tonight, and if we're lucky we may have company before mornin'."

It was a long haul for men who had been in the saddle most of the day. Jim and Oats thought nothing of it, and old Kize offered no complaint.

Though the moon was high by the time they put their broncs into Touchstone, the passage was so narrow and the walls rose so sheer that only a thin shaft of moonlight found its way down to the floor of the canyon. They moved cautiously, aware that the confining walls of the deep cavern magnified the slightest sound and sent its warning ahead of them.

The sheriff took the lead. Jim and Oats strung out behind him, riding in single file. This narrow, twisting defile through the Buckskins ran on and on for a long two miles before it opened on the desert wastes of the Owyhee and the Red Buttes beyond.

Time was not of the essence now; they moved slowly, advancing a hundred yards and then pulling up to test the stillness of the night and catalogue every sound the canyon breeze brought to their ears. Fragments of rock slid down from the crumbling rim, bounding high after striking the floor and sending up a great din that echoed and re-echoed until its receding thunder died away in the far reaches of the canyon. Where they could they rode in the pitch-blackness close to the walls, but it was not always possible to avoid the thin shaft of moonlight that filtered down from above.

At one pause Kize waved Jim and Oats to his side.

"No point in goin' all the way through," he told them. "She widens out a bit beyond. We'll go that far and hole up there and wait the night out."

They began another slow advance and had just swung around a bend when Kize waved them up again.

"Listen to that!" he commanded, rising in his stirrups. "That's cows, and they're bein' run! I can tell by the way they're bellerin'!"

The distant rumble grew in volume with every passing moment.

"We better drop back," Jim advised. "This is a tough spot to be caught in. If those cows are spooked up they'll run us down!"

"No, sir!" Kize rapped. "We've hit the jackpot, and I ain't droppin' back! Stands to reason this can't be more'n a couple dozen head. If we have to we can turn 'em with our guns."

The plunging hoofbeats swelled to rumbling thunder, the canyon walls throwing the sound back and forth until it seemed that an avalanche of cattle was bearing down on them. Oats cursed his nervous bronc and fingered his gun. The other horses, range-wise, too, rolled their eyes, having no stomach for these close quarters.

The flat crack of coiled ropes and the shouting of the men who were hazing the cows through Touchstone pierced the din of hoofs and bellowing.

Jim consciously braced himself for the onslaught. He felt that what they were doing was foolhardy, however they made out. He glanced at Kize, a black silhouette against the streak of moonlight, and realized that it was useless to attempt to dissuade him now.

A moment more and they could see the frenzied steers, tails up and heads down, charging toward them, their horns scraping the walls and flashing wickedly in the sliver of moonlight.

"Use yore guns!" Kize yelled. "Keep 'em buckin'!"

Belatedly he realized that their predicament was more serious than he had anticipated.

The night was suddenly made hideous with the crashing of their gunfire. The flashes as much as the noise put terror in the surprised cows. The ones in the lead tried to check their mad rush, but were pushed on by those that followed.

Quickly reloading their guns, the three men began another fusillade. It had the desired effect, but the milling, slithering herd was not thirty feet away when it ground to a momentary halt and then began doubling back up the canyon, driving the rustlers ahead of it.

"Handed them gents a surprise!" Oats shouted gleefully. "They better not stop fannin' their broncs till they hit the Owyhee!"

The sheriff ordered them to take up the pursuit. The tables were turned now, and they drove the panic-stricken steers ahead of them without thought of life or limb, firing over their heads and using their voices in a wild whooping that would have done credit to an Indian.

The surprise of the four rustlers was complete, too. They had been using Touchstone for weeks and had taken its safety for granted. Flight was imperative now, and without exchanging a shot they turned their horses and soon drew away from the stampeding steers. They had a rope corral in Touchstone Canyon. They reached it in the course of a mile, let themselves through, and were gone long before their pursuers, bovine and human, came in sight.

When the cows came up against the barrier they ground to a halt. Kize and his deputies surmised the reason. Investigation proved them correct.

"We can get through if you want to go on," Jim remarked. Kize shook his head.

"No use; we couldn't overhaul 'em now." A cow stood where the moonlight struck it. He had a look at the brand. "Hank Dorn's stuff," he announced. "About thirty head. They didn't put on any weight tonight," he added dryly. "We'll have to stay with them till mornin'. One of you can ride over to Box D and tell Hank to pick 'em up."

They pulled the saddles off their horses and settled down to spending the rest of the night in the canyon, each to take a turn at standing guard while the others slept.

"It's tough to lose those birds when we was as close to them as that," Oats declared. "I wonder who they was."

"I reckon we know," Kize muttered. "Catchin' them here spells Bar 66 in letters a foot high to me. Mebbe we'll be able to pick up somethin' in the mornin' that'll knock any guesswork out of it."

In the morning they found numerous cigarette butts and the ashes of several small fires, evidence that the corral had been used on previous occasions. Jim picked up a frayed and faded hatband. It could have lain there for years and was hardly to be regarded as a clue.

"When we get out of the canyon are we going to Bar 66 for a face up?" he asked.

Kize studied him thoughtfully for a moment. "Would that be yore idea of the smart thing to do?"

"I don't know as it would. Those fellows last night got away unseen and unhurt. They won't come this way again, but they'll find another way and keep playing their game if we hold off and let them get the idea that they're not suspected. That might be the smart thing to do; it'll give us another chance at them. Flush your birds before you've got them dead to rights and you're apt to lose them."

Kize wagged his head. "That's exactly how I figger it. I'm glad you agree with me. We can purty near call our shots now. We'll give these gents all the rope they require and see if we can't move in on the headman."

"Morgan?"

"Morgan! Who else?"

Chapter Seven

BARELY LEGAL BEEF

Kize sought out Otis Longyear on reaching town and told him about the brush with the rustlers in Touchstone. He knew he wasn't giving anything away that there was any hope of holding back; if no one else talked, Henry Dorn would.

"Hank came through for us at the meetin'," he told Longyear. "This sorta squares us with him. He was mighty pleased to git his cows back."

"I imagine he was," the district attorney agreed. "If it does nothing else, it shows him you're on the job. I hope he talks it up to the other members of the board. They took my word for it day before yesterday that we'd come through with something directly. They'll hold us to it."

"I know," Kize acknowledged. "This could have been it, if we'd snagged those fellas."

"You haven't any idea who they are?"

The sheriff shook his head. "It was pitch-black in the canyon. We heard 'em yellin', but with all that noise you couldn't recognize a voice. But don't you worry, Otis; I'll stamp out' the rustlin'. I got some ideas about it."

As usual, Longyear tried to draw him out and

had no success. Kize left the courthouse to discover that news of the encounter had already reached town. It was time for the *Enterprise* to be off the press, but it was not yet on the street. He took it for granted that Iris had caught the paper at the last minute and was holding it up to include the Touchstone Canyon story.

Judge Messenger came down the steps a moment later and called him back. They were friends of long standing. "What you and Otis had to say at the board meeting got back to me in a roundabout way," the judge said. "It's encouraging to know you're making some progress. I'd like to believe we're getting to the end of all this wholesale killing and robbery."

"So would I," Kize told him. "But that's more than I can promise you, Horace. The evidence is pilin' up against certain parties. One of these days we'll pull the roof down on 'em."

They talked for a few minutes. The boys who delivered the *Enterprise* had got their papers and were running up the street by the time Kize reached the corner. He got a copy and found a brief account of the Touchstone Canyon affair on the front page. The story was substantially correct and disclosed nothing that he wanted to hold back. He reached his office a few minutes later and found Iris and Jim there.

"Take your chair, Dad," she urged, getting up. "I'll sit on the desk." She gave him a pecking kiss. "I tried to locate you. Jim told me you were in the courthouse with Otis."

"So I was," he said, his frown hiding his great pride in her. "I just had a look at the paper. Where'd you git your story?"

"Young Wilbur Rainey came in from Cabin Creek with the news. I got what I could from him. When I couldn't find you I buttonholed him. Did I say too much?"

"No, it's all right."

"I'm glad to hear that," she observed with mock relief. "I'd hate to be in bad with both of you. Jim's just been reading me the riot act for my editorial on that nasty business at Spanish Ford yesterday morning."

"Hunh!" Kize snorted suspiciously. "I ain't seen that yet."

"Read it," Jim advised, "and you'll agree with me that she ought to be spanked."

Kize snatched up the *Enterprise* and turned to the editorial page. The article bitterly attacked Wild Bill Mullhall for manhandling a defenseless cripple. It wanted to know what had become of Western manhood that once had been proud to succor the weak and the helpless. A long list of Mullhall's offenses and brutalities was recorded. *How much longer will the community tolerate the presence of this man?* it asked. *Surely not for long,* it concluded.

"Good grief!" Kize exploded, slapping the

paper down on his desk with an angry bang. "Iris, that's the craziest thing you ever did! It plays right into the hands of the skunks we're tryin' to run down! Shore he beat up Ben Riley and half kicked the life out of him, but the whole thing was framed! They wanted to git Bill Mullhall out on the end of a limb and whip up feelin' against him, and, by grab, you've done yore dangest to help 'em out!"

Iris got down from the desk. "If you'll stop shouting at me and explain what you mean I'll try to understand," she exclaimed, white spots of indignation in her cheeks.

"You needn't git on yore high horse," Kize protested. "Jim and me have tried to set you straight, but you won't listen. You've got it into yore head that Bill Mullhall is responsible for what you call this 'reign of terror,' and you're not goin' to be talked out of it. I ain't makin' no excuses for him; he's everythin' you say he is. But if he wasn't around, things would be worse than they are; the gang that's in the saddle is more afraid of him than the law. He knows what the setup is, and they know that he knows. He's got that bunch shakin' in their boots, and not only because he can call the turn on 'em. What's really got 'em scared is that he may move in on their game. That's why they're out to git rid of him. By gravy, they won't git away with it if I can help it! Bill Mullhall is mighty valuable to me!"

"It's too bad you waited until now to let me know these things," Iris told him. She was both chagrined and annoyed.

"It's a peculiar situation—me the sheriff and you the editor of the paper," Kize grumbled. "You've always respected my confidence, but, with things as bad as they are, I figgered you might be safer the less you knew. You lay off of Bill Mullhall. And forgit whatever I may have said about him."

"No, I want a fuller explanation than that before I make any promises," she insisted. "Can't the two of you be frank with me for once? You know it's off the record. You said what happened at Spanish Ford was arranged. I want to know what you meant by that."

She turned appealingly to Jim.

"She's right," said he. "You've gone so far, Kize, you might as well tell her the rest."

The sheriff was not easily persuaded to disclose the few facts and multiple suspicions that pointed to Little Ben Riley as the informer for the gang that was behind the robberies and murders that had plagued the community for weeks. In the end he did, and Iris was properly amazed and humbled. She had known the man almost from the day of his arrival in Rock Creek three years ago. He had come up from Carson City or some town in Washoe Valley and gone to work as a clerk in the post office. She had seen and talked with him every day until he was transferred to the branch office at Spanish Ford.

"It's incredible," she said. "Little Ben was always so kind and obliging. I couldn't help liking him."

"A lot of people like him," Jim remarked. "They'll be as surprised as you are when the showdown comes. I'm certain he's had a finger in every one of these killings. He's the last man in the world you'd suspect of being a crook. That's what makes him so dangerous. I don't question for a moment that Tom Yancey confided in him that he was coming to town to try and spot the men who killed Foraker. You can charge that murder up to him."

These disclosures left Iris aghast. "I felt all along that this wave of crime didn't have you as baffled as you pretended," she said. "But I had no idea that you had got as far as this—and, of course, you're not telling me everything even now. Dad, are you ready to break this whole mess wide open?"

"No, I wouldn't say that!" Kize declared emphatically. "We've got a long ways to go. If you want to help things along, don't have any more to say against Mullhall."

"You've got my word on that," she promised. "I doubt that the editorial will have any great effect one way or the other, but I'm willing to do anything I can about it, short of printing a retraction."

She heard Jim chuckling softly. She turned around to him quickly, her eyes flashing danger signals. "What did I say that was so amusing?" she demanded.

"I was just thinking about Bill and a retraction. He may demand one. What'll you do, Iris, if he comes storming in tomorrow morning and threatens to tear the place apart unless he gets satisfaction?"

"Let him come," she replied with a little toss of her head. "I'm not the least bit afraid of Wild Bill Mullhall. I'll handle him."

"You might at that," he conceded. "They say Bill's just pie for a pretty girl. Come, Iris, I was only having a little fun with you. If I know him, he'll be delighted to find that he's so important that the *Enterprise* has to devote its editorial column to him. If the two of you are going home I'll walk along with you as far as my place. What time tomorrow evening do you want us to show up?"

"Don't make it any later than a quarter to seven," she replied. "That'll give me time to bake a cake after I get home from the office. There'll be just Oats, you and Dan Corbett, and the two of us. I'll have Mrs. Corey come and get the roast started. It's cool on the back porch these evenings. I'll set the table there. Dan's going to bring some champagne. After dinner we'll have a fast little game of stud."

"What's the occasion for all the festivities—invitin' the boys and Doc Corbett to the house?" Kize inquired.

"Your birthday, as if you didn't know. I'd hear from you if I ever forgot."

Kize protested that she shouldn't have bothered. But he was pleased. "You work all day, Iris. It's askin' too much to have you rush home and fix a big dinner."

"Don't worry about that, Dad. You just see to it that you don't light out for the Bend or somewhere at the last minute and leave me with a three-layer cake and a big roast in the oven."

Kize received a letter from Ike Burch postmarked Reno the following morning. Burch wrote that he was going to work for the Adelaide Mining Company at Golconda and could be reached there at any time.

"That sounds like he's goin' to be on the level with me," the sheriff said to Jim and Oats. "He wouldn't have wrote if he had any idea of givin' me the slip. I'll drop him a line jest to let him know I appreciate the courtesy."

He got out pen and paper. When he had his letter finished he took it to the post office. He had instructed his deputies to visit the restaurants and butcher shops and make sure that the new ordinance pertaining to the sale of beef was not being violated. He had reserved the Maverick

Hotel for his own inspection. Using the alley at the rear of the post office, he reached the back of the hotel unnoticed.

Across the alley from the kitchen stood the small brick building, recently completed, in which meats and other perishable foods were stored until needed. Sounds from the storeroom proclaimed that some activity was going on within. He pushed through the heavy door and found two of the hotel's kitchen crew busily cutting up a side of beef. On the meat rack six dressed halves were hanging. Though the Maverick was serving several hundred meals a day, it could not be using as much beef as this. It confirmed Kize's suspicion that Morgan was quietly supplying some of the other restaurants in town.

The two men had stopped working. They saw the sheriff run a hand over the sides of beef. He found them warm enough to suggest that they had just been brought in.

"This stuff hasn't been hangin' long," he said. "Where did it come from?"

"The ranch," one of the men answered. He was a sallow-faced Greek. Picking up a steel, he began to sharpen a long wicked-looking knife, his manner suggesting that it was for a distinctly unpleasant purpose.

"This beef has been out in the sun till a few minutes ago," Kize growled. "You fellas ain't had time to jerk the hides. It came in fully dressed, didn't it?"

The Greek shrugged. "We justa work here. Suppose you spik to Meester Morg'."

"Don't give me none of yore insolence!" the old man whipped back. "I'll speak to you, and you'll give me a straight answer!" He had a look about the room and failed to find any hides. "What did you do with 'em?" he demanded. "Or didn't they even bother to bring 'em in?"

"You spik wit' de boss," the Greek repeated less truculently.

"By grab, I will!" Kize burst out angrily. "Stop what yo're doin'; I'm seizin' this beef!"

He started for the door. It opened before he reached it, and Morgan, resplendent in mauve weskit this morning, walked in. He appeared undisturbed by the sheriff's hostile attitude.

"One of my dishwashers told me you were back here," he said coolly. "What seems to be the trouble?"

"This beef," Kize told him. "You know the law. Yo're violating the old ordinance as well as the new; you can't show hides for this stuff."

"That's correct, but I'm not violating any law, Kize. Both of them relate to the sale of beef. I'm not offering anything for sale; I'm slaughtering my own cattle, bringing it to town, and putting it in my cooler to serve in my dining-room as needed. To be sure I was right about it I got some legal advice. Pat Holman is as good a lawyer as there is in town. He tells me I'm in the clear."

Kize didn't attempt to conceal his annoyance. "Mebbe there *is* a loophole in the law. If so, I'll see that it's plugged up in a hurry. Everyone knows why the ordinances was passed and are willin' to abide by 'em. To say the least, it seems mighty peculiar that you'd seek legal advice to help you git around them. You got cattle runnin' on the open range. I'd think you'd be interested in doin' what you can to help us put an end to the rustlin'."

"You bet I'm interested in breaking it up," Con averred. "I'm not standing in your way. It saves me fifty dollars a week to slaughter what beef I need at the ranch and pull the hides on the spot. My kitchen crew is overworked as it is. If I had to go to extra work with the beef I'd have to hire a couple more men. And where you going to get men in this town? They want three bucks a day and grub just for washing dishes. Besides, I haven't any room; the cooler isn't half big enough for my needs."

Kize thought he saw an opportunity to drive Morgan into a corner, and he pounced on it. "If you need room," he said, "why fill it up with beef? You could have a carcass sent in every couple days. How long will all this run you?"

Morgan wanted to say three or four days, but

he saw the trap. It told him as plainly as though it had been shouted from the housetops that he was suspect. There had been other incidents that cried a warning even before the slaying of Tom Yancey. This was all the confirmation he needed.

"It'll carry me two or three weeks," he said, knowing that he was closing the door on any further activity for that time. The whole question of what to do about Kize Farraday was rapidly coming to a head in Morgan's mind. Chuck Silvey was suspect, too. Something would have to be done about him. "If you think there's anything queer about this beef why don't you go out to the ranch and tell Legrand you want to look things over?"

Kize bristled at this piece of advice. "If I have any occasion to look yore ranch over I'll manage it without havin' to consult yore foreman. You may be legally in the clear as far as the ordinances go; I know they was drawn hastily. I'll git an interpretation from Longyear. If they need fixin' up, the board can do it at the next meetin'. All I'm supposed to do is enforce the laws; I don't write 'em. If Longyear tells me to confiscate this beef and file a charge against you I'll have to do it."

"He won't tell you anything of the sort."

"Mebbe not. That ain't goin' to stop some liftin' of eyebrows in yore direction, Con. You may be doin' business with yoreself as you say, but a lot of folks ain't goin' to see it that way; talk will start that you're coverin' up somethin'."

Con drew himself up in wrathful indignation. "Is that your way of hinting that this beef is rustled?"

"I'm not hintin' at anythin'. I'm only tellin' you what the talk's goin' to be, and you know when gossip of that sort gits goin' it's hard to stop—no matter how innocent a man may be. Mebbe you can afford it. Mebbe you don't care."

His fate was sealed as far as Morgan was concerned. If the latter now pretended to be placated, it was only acting.

"We've always been friends, Kize," he declared with the air of one who is being magnanimous. "There's no reason why we should have any trouble now. As you say, there'll be talk if I buck the ordinance. I don't usually pay any attention to that sort of stuff. But I'm not going to be a dog in the manger about this; I'll play it your way and charge up the extra expense to experience."

Kize wasn't fooled by this sudden about-face, but he had to pretend to be pleased. "That's decent of you," he declared. "It's the sensible way to look at it."

"What about this beef?" Con asked. "Do you want me to send it back to the ranch?"

"No, it would spoil. Use it up and just be sure the next lot comes in with the hair on." He told the Greek and the other man to go on with their work. With Con he crossed the alley to the hotel, and they walked through the empty dining-room together. Halfway Con stopped, and after making sure they were quite alone he said confidentially, "I hear Chuck Silvey was run out of Spanish Ford the day before yesterday. The way it was told to me, you and your deputies saved his bacon."

"Yeh," Kize muttered, wondering what this was leading up to. "That crowd sounded real ugly." Intent on doing a little maneuvering of his own, he added, "We pulled out right behind him and made shore he wasn't bein' followed. The last we saw of him, he was cuttin' across to yore place on the south fork. He spends a lot of his time on the ranch."

He expected Morgan to deny it. The denial came in a strange way, and the old man was wholly unprepared for it.

"He doesn't spend as much time on my ranch as he'd like to have you think."

Under his hooded brows Kize rifled a fierce searching glance at him. "What do you expect me to make of that?" he jerked out.

"Whatever you please," was Con's flinty answer. "He's had me over a barrel long enough. That business at Montero's place opened my eyes. Watch Dinwiddie's Hole."

Kize spent the rest of the morning thinking it over. He thought he knew why Morgan was tossing Silvey to the wolves. As for Dinwiddie's Hole, it was a lonely, brush-clogged box canyon above the headwaters of the south fork.

"It's a likely spot," he muttered to himself. "I'll have a look at it."

Jim came in and recognized the signs of deep concentration in him. "What have you got on your mind now?" he asked,

"Nothin'," Kize grumbled. "Jest puttin' two and two together."

Chapter Eight

BLOODSTAINED SADDLE

Jim and Oats had found no one violating the new ordinance. When Kize related his experience with Con Morgan they gathered around him, full of questions. He intentionally omitted repeating everything that had been said about Chuck Silvey.

"There wasn't a hide in the place. That beef had been brought in ready to be cut up," he told them. "Con didn't make any bones about it."

Jim found a copy of the law and read it carefully. "I believe Morgan's right. Listen to this. 'No beef steer shall be offered for sale, or bartered, or otherwise used in trade.' It doesn't forbid a man doing business with himself. You couldn't ask Morgan to send a piece of hide to the table with every steak he serves. What gets me is why he backed down—that's if he really is the boss man."

Oats looked up, puzzled. "Why do you say that? If he's smart enough to run this assortment of thieves and cutthroats, you got to figger he knows we're makin' some progress. He may think it's time for him to pull in his horns a bit."

"No," Jim demurred, "it's always a sign of

weakness to back down when you find the going getting a little rough. Morgan knows that's the way we'd see it, and it would be the last thing he'd do. He's got something else up his sleeve. Of course, he may be only the number-two man. Have you thought of that, Kize?"

"I've thought of it," the sheriff said grumpily. "It never gits me anywhere. I can't put my finger on any character in these parts who could fill that pair of shoes, unless it's Wild Bill, and I know damn well that it ain't him."

He ran into Mullhall on the street just before noon. The latter was as sober as he ever was. He greeted Kize with apparent good will.

"That girl of yours sure knows how to sell her papers," he declared with a harsh chuckle. "She sure ripped hell out of me, didn't she?"

"I don't tell her what to write," the old man replied. "She does her own thinkin', and I do mine. But I do agree with one thing she wrote, though not for the same reason. It was outright foolish of you to tear into Little Ben that way. You was only giving the element that's down on you somethin' they can git their teeth into. Why did you slam him around like that, Bill?"

"Because he's just like that with certain parties that'd like to see me run out." He held up two fingers of his right hand and entwined them. "I got his play right away. It made me so damn mad I wanted to kill him. You tell your daughter that if he comes at me again I'll bring her his ears for a souvenir."

Wild Bill's broad pock-marked face was expressionless and his eyes as empty as an Indian's as he looked down at Kize, measuring the effect of the tip he had given him about Little Ben Riley. "I see I wasn't tellin' you anythin' you didn't know," he said fiercely.

"I'm obliged jest the same," the old man told him.

At that moment events were about to transpire on the trail across the Blue Meadows from Rustlers' Bend close to where it cut into the Rock Creek Road that were to call for more headlines. The principal actor, as events were to show, was one Rawhide Smith.

Rawhide Smith had been around a long time. He could truthfully call himself Rock Creek's oldest citizen, which he often did. For the past twenty years he had subsisted on his army pension and the charity of his granddaughter's husband. As a scout he had served through the campaigns against the Paiutes and farther north in the war with Bannocks. He was six feet tall in his bare feet and, though he was an octogenarian, still straight as a ramrod and tough as bullhide.

Though he had no demands on his time and could have been one of the first to stake a claim in the Bend, he had scoffed at what he called the fools who rushed in. After every foot of likely-looking ground had been pre-empted he put in an appearance and announced that he was going to locate a claim. On sounding him out and discovering that he knew nothing about placering, several loungers at Johnnie Montero's then saloon had advised him in jest to go up the bank above the gravel bars and try his luck there.

That Rawhide Smith did and, to the amazement of all, struck it rich. He kept a rifle handy, did not bother to erect a tent or other shelter, and worked his claim in good weather and bad. Every evening, rifle on his shoulder, he marched into Johnnie's place and turned over to him the proceeds of the day's work for safe forwarding to Rock Creek. Johnnie soon found it a nuisance. But do a Basque a favor, and he never forgets. Rawhide Smith had befriended Johnnie's people when they first came to Nevada and found themselves unwanted. So he kept his bargain with Rawhide.

The pocket which the old man had so miraculously discovered could not hold out forever. Johnnie had seen Rawhide's poke grow lighter and lighter until it shrank to less than an ounce a day. He advised him to quit, for Rawhide was a rich man. But Rawhide had hung on. For the past ten days he had not bothered to deposit his dust with Johnnie. It was safe enough with him, he said; nobody was interested in robbing a man of such a trifling amount.

This morning he had appeared at the store with the word that he was pulling out. He had no need of leaving a forwarding address for his mail; he never received any letters. Waving Johnnie good-by, he had taken the trail across the Blue Meadows, his rifle on his shoulder and a small pack on his back, looking exactly as he had on the day when he first appeared at Spanish Ford.

All had gone well with him until he neared the road. There a masked man waited, his .44 ready. A second before he stepped out and called on him to throw up his hands Rawhide saw him. The old man threw up his rifle, not his hands, and put his bullet squarely between the bandit's eyes. Removing the mask, he saw that his assailant was Ad Jenkins, who at varying intervals worked an unproductive claim, or pretended to, but was better known as Chuck Silvey's boon companion.

The news was not long in reaching town. Oats brought it to the office. Kize and Jim were frankly delighted.

"Score one for our side, even if we didn't get him," the latter exclaimed. "Ad Jenkins. That gives us another string on Silvey; they did their playing together, and I'm dead sure they killed together. If we ever get the whole story on who killed Jeff Foraker we'll find it was that pair."

"I'll go along with you on that," said Kize.

"You and Oats git up there as soon as you can. You better take the coroner with you. He can arrange about having the body brought in. Search it carefully; you may be lucky enough to find some evidence on him that we can use."

For him to stay behind was unusual. Jim was instantly suspicious. "Why you sending us up alone?" he asked. "I swear, you're goin' after something on your own as soon as you get rid of us. You've been acting peculiar all morning."

"Peculiar, my foot!" Kize snorted disgustedly. "Iris been at you to keep an eye on me?"

"I don't know about that," Jim retorted. "It'd be too bad if she worried a little about you now and then, wouldn't it?"

"That's all right—if it don't go too far. I don't need nobody steppin' on my heels all the time. Good grief! If the two of you have yore way about it you'll have me in a wheelchair by the time my next birthday rolls around!"

Kize was pouring it on for a purpose, not wanting to have any questions asked about what he was bent on doing that afternoon.

"The two of you git up to the Blue Meadows," he repeated. "You don't need me to help you handle that business. I got somethin' I want to look into. Won't take me long; I'll be right here when you git back."

"All right, but you watch your p's and q's," Jim scolded. "We should be back by five. You see

113

that you are. Don't you spoil the evening for Iris like you did last year—she had the dinner in and out of the oven two or three times before you finally showed up."

Since the old man's interest in having a look at Dinwiddie's Hole and the adjacent country sprang solely from the tip Con Morgan had given him, he must have had some reason to believe it a dangerous mission. Why he felt justified in undertaking it alone is difficult to understand, unless it can be charged to perverseness or a conviction that it would result in the complete exposure of the outlaw ring and, having accomplished it singlehanded, silence his critics and permit him to retire in a blaze of glory.

By way of Rustlers' Bend and Spanish Ford it was fully twenty-five miles to Dinwiddie's Hole. It was a long, roundabout way. There was no road directly east from town, but by taking to the hills and cutting through the lava beds beyond, a horseman could reach the Hole in an hour's riding.

Kize waited only until he was sure his deputies had left with Shep Failes, the coroner, for the Blue Meadows. He threw a saddle on his favorite bronc then, and a few minutes later he jogged across the Rock Creek bridge at the head of the main street and struck off to the east.

The *Enterprise* had received news of Rawhide Smith's slaying of Ad Jenkins. Iris was writing the story when she saw Jim and Oats Ollinger ride by. They had Shep Failes with them. Their destination appeared obvious. She wondered why her father wasn't accompanying them, but when Kize passed a few minutes later she took it for granted that he was on his way to overtake them and she thought no more about it, other than to speculate on how late they would be getting back.

The paper was on the press and she was clearing her desk so that she might get away early when Henry Hustis, the owner of the *Enterprise*, put his head in the door. "Hold on to your hat, Iris," he said. "I've got a surprise for you."

"Good heavens, you don't mean you're raising my salary, Henry?" she returned laughingly.

"I don't know about the raise, but it looks as though someone else will be paying it." He lowered his voice to add, "I've been offered a good price for the *Enterprise*. If we can work out a deal with you I'm going to let it go."

An incredulous expression settled on Iris's young face. Hustis had talked for several years about selling the paper and moving down to California where his wife's people lived. But that was before the *Enterprise* had begun to show a profit. For him to sell now came as a shocking surprise.

"You might have given me some warning," she protested.

"I didn't have warning myself," Hustis replied.

"I mentioned a figure I'd take several days ago, but it was just one of those casual conversations, I thought, and I never expected anything to come of it. A few minutes ago he walks in and says he's ready to make a deal. It won't make any difference to you, Iris; he wants you to stay on as editor. In fact he makes that one of the conditions in buying the paper."

"That's nice of him," she murmured. "It's someone from out of town, of course."

"No—Con Morgan."

"Con Morgan?" Iris straightened up as though she had just received an electric shock. "Good Lord, no! Not that man, Henry!"

Hustis hurriedly closed the office door. "Keep your voice down—he'll hear you!" he burst out, as excited as she, though not for the same reason. "What's wrong with Con Morgan?"

"It's the most outrageous thing I ever heard of—that—that—" She couldn't finish what she wanted to say without violating the confidence her father and Jim had reposed in her. "I—I'm sorry I said anything at all," she added lamely. "If he takes over he'll have to hire himself a new editor; I couldn't work for him."

"Because he sells whisky and takes a rake-off on some gambling? That's terribly naïve of you, Iris!" Hustis accused bitterly, fearful that Farraday stubbornness, with which he had had some experience, would cost him the sale. "Con's one of the most popular men in Rock Creek. I never heard anyone say anything against him; he's always been a square shooter. Don't wreck this deal for me, Iris. Why can't you go on?"

"Because I know how he'd want the *Enterprise* run—how I'd be told what to write and how it was to be slanted. Did he say anything about the Mullhall editorial?"

"Just casually. He thought it was fine. Con's public-spirited; he's for anything that's for the good of the community."

Con's favorable reaction to the editorial gave Iris her cue. It made his purpose in purchasing the *Enterprise* very plain.

"You're all wrong about being told where to head in," Hustis pressed on. "Not five minutes ago Con told me that he knew nothing about publishing a newspaper and that he wants you to take charge—combine your duties and mine and run the paper as you think best. It'll mean more money for you, Iris. There's no reason why you can't try it out for a month or two. If it doesn't work out your way you can always quit. But don't give it a flat turndown. Come on up in front and hear what Morgan has to say. That's the least you can do."

She was finally persuaded, but not in response to urging. Any idea that Morgan would refuse to go through with the deal unless her services were included was absurd to her. Being convinced of his purpose in purchasing the paper, she took it for granted that if she resigned he would bring in an editor of his own. In that event there would be nothing to stop Morgan from launching an all-out campaign against Mullhall. If she remained on the job she could protect her father's interests in some degree. Iris needed no other argument.

Con wore a coat this afternoon, formal attire for him. He knew how to be courteous, and he put his best foot forward with her. "I hope you've considered my proposition favorably, Miss Farraday."

"Yes and no," she answered. "I've had a free hand here, and I've tried to make the *Enterprise* a strong weapon for law and order. I've stepped on some people's toes, but I've always had evidence to justify my stand. That's the only way I can work. If I'm to consider staying on, it will have to be on the explicit understanding that I am to handle the news and the editorial page as I see fit."

"Of course!" Con assured her. "You're a courageous young woman, Miss Farraday. I want the paper to be run in the best interest of the community and, naturally, to show a profit. I know you can do it. It's not my intention to pop in here and tell you what to write and how to write it. I want you to call a spade a spade. That goes," he added with a grin that made little impression on his cavernous countenance, "even if you find yourself gunning for me."

His protestations, uttered with a ring of sincerity, failed to have any effect on Iris. It was talk and nothing more than talk, she believed. It would not be long, she was sure, before he tried to force her hand. She was secretly resolved to go through with it, however, and when she left Con and Hustis to conclude their arrangement she had given her promise to stay with the *Enterprise.*

She had left for home before Jim and Oats got back to town. They had found a rather large amount of currency on Ad Jenkins, as well as several letters. The letters contained nothing of an incriminating nature against the dead man or anyone else. Otherwise, the deputies had learned nothing beyond the facts they had when they left for the Blue Meadows.

It was after five, and Kize was not at the office. They were not immediately anxious about him, but when half past five came and he did not put in an appearance Jim went down to the barn to see if one of the old man's string of broncs was missing. What he found sent him hurrying back to the office.

"The sorrel mare's gone," he told Oats. "That means he ain't around town. Grab your hat; we'll go up the street and try to find out what's become of him."

They had tried the hotel and several saloons without result when they met the marshal.

"Yeh, I saw him about half past two," Cap told

them. "When I saw him ridin' out I figgered he was bound for the Meadows."

"He crossed the bridge, eh?" Jim asked.

"I dunno. The Hoskin boy was fishin' there all afternoon. He could tell yuh."

They went off in search of Dale Hoskin. He told them he had seen the sheriff turn eastward soon after crossing the creek.

"He was riding old Jinny," he said. "You know the trail old man Revell used when he had a cabin in the Squaw Hills. That's the way he was heading."

It posed a question that neither Jim nor Oats could answer.

"It gets me!" the latter declared soberly. "I don't know of anythin' in the Squaw Hills that would interest him. Maybe he was just takin' a short cut to 'where he was goin'.'"

This struck Jim as a very logical observation. In his mind's eye he mapped out the Squaw Hills and the country beyond. Once through the hills, a man would have the lava beds, the headwaters of the south fork, Dinwiddie's Hole, and, not too far to the north, Morgan's Bar 66 ranch ahead of him. That was enough for Jim. He discussed it with Oats, and they were of one mind about it.

"Sure as shootin', he lit out to have a look at Morgan's spread." Oats was positive. "An hour's ridin' each way would do it. That's why he told us he'd bc back in the office by five."

"I hope there's nothing wrong," young Hoskin said.

"So do we," Jim answered. He thanked the boy, and they turned back into town, their faces grave.

"Jim—the old man's run into trouble." Oats had seldom sounded so grim. "We'll have to go out lookin' for him. Waitin' ain't goin' to make the job any easier. The best thing we can do is to organize a searchin' party and get started."

Jim shook his head. "We'll wait till half past six before we throw Iris into a panic and go out looking for him. There's still time for him to show up."

"Yeh," Oats agreed. Each knew the other was convinced to the contrary.

They stopped in front of Dr. Corbett's house, and Jim went in. Corbett had his office and waiting-room on the ground floor. The rest of the frame building had been transformed into a hospital of sorts, Rock Creek having no other facilities of that nature.

"I was just getting ready to leave," was the young doctor's greeting. He gave Jim a second look. "What's the matter with you?" he asked banteringly. "Aren't you dressing up a bit for the party? You haven't even shaved."

"Dan—Kize is missing."

"What!" Lord's gravity eloquently expressed the seriousness with which he regarded the situation. It pulled Corbett to his feet, his deep and immediate concern evident.

Jim hurriedly explained himself. He had no hesitancy in speaking frankly. No one—not even Iris—had been so freely taken into their confidence as Corbett, who had a keen interest in the scientific phases of criminal investigation. His laboratory was too inadequate to promise much, but his microscope had provided them with some amazing bits of information.

"He wanted to get back early for a couple reasons," Jim continued. "If he got in early he wouldn't have to explain where he'd been. And it's his birthday; he wouldn't want to spoil things for Iris. A lot of things could have happened to upset his calculations; he may be all right. Somehow I can't believe it, Dan."

"You feel sure that he set out for Bar 66?" Corbett knew why Morgan's ranch was suspect.

"I don't know what else to think," said Jim. He looked at his watch. "It's almost six-thirty. I'll give him until then."

"That'll give you a little better than an hour of daylight." Corbett walked to the window and glanced up the road in the direction of the bridge. He was a tall man, square-shouldered, with a rather plain face relieved by a pair of intelligent eyes and a strong mouth. "Jim, you want me to see Iris? It'll save you a little time."

"I wish you would, Dan. She has a lot of faith

in you. It would be foolish to try to make her think there's nothing wrong, but don't let her look at the worst side of it."

"I'll make it as easy on her as I can. You get me a horse; I'll be over to the sheriff's office before you're organized and ready to ride. I've got a feeling I better go with you. I'll bring my bag along."

It did not take Jim and Oats long to enlist a dozen men, most of them cowboys who chanced to be in town. Some left their supper untouched, others hastily gulped down a few mouthfuls and repaired to the street in front of the sheriff's office, where the posse was to rendezvous. Dr. Corbett joined them at the last moment. Jim asked at once how Iris had taken the news.

"She didn't go to pieces," Dan told him. "It hit her hard, of course, but she's like Kize—she can hold herself in. Coming this evening, of all times, made it worse."

"I blame myself," Jim muttered bitterly. "I knew he was up to something."

"You can blame yourself if you feel you must," said Dan. "Iris knows it isn't your fault. Kize ordered you and Oats to get up to the Meadows. I don't know what you could do but go; he's the boss. I stopped on the way over to ask Belle Newcomb and Carrie Brundage to go over to the house and stay with her till we get back."

A signal from Jim set the posse in motion. The gathering crowd parted to let them through. The pace quickened as they swung into the main street. The loose planks in the Rock Creek bridge set up a noisy tattoo as they thundered across.

The trail was well-defined as far as Gabe Revell's abandoned cabin. Beyond it wound through a tangle of mountain mahogany and aspens for several miles. It slowed the horses to a walk in many places. Finally the posse came out above the scrub timber and had the rocky, badly cutup Squaw Hills ahead of them. They had worked through as far as the lava beds and nest of springs that fed the south fork before the light began to fail.

After a brief parley Jim lead half of the posse in the direction of the springs; Oats began scouring the lava beds with the others. The purple afterglow was fading to deep twilight when they joined forces again. Nothing had been seen of Kize.

"It'll be black night in a few minutes," Oats remarked, stating the obvious. "If we're goin' to search out the crick bottom and have a peek in the Hole we'll have to hole up here till the moon shows."

"Why not push on to Bar 66?" one of the men asked. "They may be able to tell us somethin' there."

Oats and Corbett exchanged a quick glance

with Jim. In the gathering darkness they saw him return a firm no to their unasked question. Nothing had been said to the posse regarding the suspicions the three of them entertained against the Morgan ranch. Plainly Jim did not intend to say anything.

"We'll mark time here for half an hour," he announced. "It'll be some lighter after the early darkness fades. If we can't see what we're doing we'll wait for the moon."

They had been there only a few minutes when Oats caught the faint whinnying of a horse. He asked for quiet. The sound came again from far off to the right.

"Did you catch that, Jim?" Oats demanded excitedly.

"Sure. Sounded as though it came from over toward the Hole."

"And it sounded like old Jinny to me!" Oats whipped out, angered by the lack of Jim's perception. "What's the matter with your ears? That old mare has a funny whimper. You've heard it often enough to recognize it."

They listened again and caught the sound once more. A shiver ran down Jim Lord's spine.

"It's Jinny!" he ground out. "Come on!"

They found the faithful old mare standing where the reins had been dropped over her head. A few feet away lay Kize. Dan's brief examination was hardly necessary.

"He's dead," he muttered. "He's been dead some time; he's cold. Shot through the head."

They were gathered around the body when one of the posse cried, "Look here!"

Someone broke off a clump of dead sage and touched a match to it. It flamed brightly, and in its weird light thirty feet away they saw Chuck Silvey staring at them with sightless eyes, his saturnine face more ugly in death than it had been in life.

"Good Lord!" Oats groaned. "The two of them—they shot it out!"

"What did Silvey have against Kize?" a man asked another.

"I reckon Kize knew somethin' about that shootin' in the Maverick the other day that was too much for Chuck."

Jim heard them, but he was too stunned for the moment to care what was said. A fire was built up, the flames leaping high and lighting the grisly scene. Dan came over to Jim and put a hand on his shoulder.

"I know how you feel," he said. "It's too bad he had to go this way. They must have come on each other without warning and blazed away."

Jim shook his head grimly. "No, you're wrong, Dan! All wrong! Look at his saddle. Bloodstains on it. You know that slug killed him instantly. He never got off his horse. This was a trap, and he rode into it!"

126

Chapter Nine

TELLTALE BULLETS

The new Methodist church was not half big enough to accommodate the throngs that came to pay their last respects to Kize Farraday. It could not be said of him that he had been unappreciated in life. But he had been criticized by many of late; others had taken him for granted—he had held down his job so long—and apparently expected him to go on forever. Now that he was gone, his loss seemed irreparable.

With Dan Corbett's help and the courageous assistance of Iris, Jim saw the old man placed to rest with the public believing that Silvey and Kize had died in a gun duel. The county commissioners had assembled hurriedly and appointed Jim to fill out the old man's unexpired term. Kize had held back every bit of information and evidence that he could on the theory that it would jell sooner or later and enable him to round up the whole outlaw ring in one spectacular move. Jim was determined to proceed on that line, believing it promised more than any other course he might pursue. Accordingly he had given the gang every reason to believe that he had been completely taken in by the ruse they had used in killing Kize and Silvey.

He had not attempted to deceive Iris. For her, knowing what she knew, it had tested her courage to the limit to write what she did about the double slaying. Her first reaction was to go to her desk and write a story that would openly accuse Con Morgan of what she believed was his part in the killing of her father, see it printed and circulated before he could prevent it, or, short of that, never to go near the *Enterprise* again. Only Jim's insistence that she go on, keeping what he had told her to herself, had persuaded her.

After the funeral Dan and Jim rode home from the cemetery with her. Morgan had been one of the mourners. Iris resented it hotly.

"If he had even a spark of decency he would have kept away."

"Everyone else was there; if he had stayed away it would have called attention to himself," Corbett pointed out.

"Of course," Jim agreed. "He's got an airtight alibi—he was talking to you and Hustis as late as four o'clock that afternoon—but that's not going to stop him from being cagey. I'm sure he doesn't know how close we've moved in on him."

"It's going to set you back, losing Dad," said Iris. "He must have taken some secrets with him."

"He took one that I'd give an arm to know. When he talked with Morgan that morning something was said that sent him up to Dinwiddie's Hole in the afternoon. It could have been a tip-off or something Morgan let slip accidentally."

"What kind of a tip?" Dan inquired.

"That he'd find something interesting up there."

The doctor shook his head. "I can't believe it; Kize was too smart to fall for anything like that—unless Con was double-crossing Silvey."

"Maybe we'll get the answer when you finish examining the slugs," Jim observed bitterly. "When will you be ready to say something, Dan?"

"This evening. You and Oats drop in anytime after eight. Are the two of you going to go it alone?"

"For the present. The commissioners authorized me to hire another man, but I don't believe I will. I've spoken to Joe Sherdell and three or four others. They've promised that I can call on them at a moment's notice and swear them in on a day-to-day basis. I think I'll play it that way."

At the house Mrs. Corey, Iris's next-door neighbor, tried to persuade her to eat something. "The icebox is bulging with salads your friends brought in, honey. I brought over a baked ham. Let me fix you something."

"Just a cup of tea," Iris said. "And thanks for everything, Martha."

Mrs. Corey appealed to Dan. "She hasn't had a thing to eat all day, Doctor. She should take some nourishment."

"She should," said Dan. "Iris, you can't go on like this. You've got to keep your strength up. A slice of ham wouldn't hurt you a bit. If I may, I'll have a piece too, Martha. I'm sure Jim will join us. Please, Iris!"

"Very well," she consented. "You've all been so kind. I don't want you to worry about me; I'm getting a firm grip on myself. I suppose I ought to go down to the shop and lay out some of the work for tomorrow."

"I won't hear of that," Jim objected strenuously. "The boys got along without you today. If you feel able to be at your desk for an hour or two tomorrow, all right."

Corbett's professional duties didn't permit him to remain more than half an hour. On leaving he said, "You get some sleep, Iris. Have you used up the tablets I left night before last?"

She shook her head. "I haven't touched them, Dan. I hate sedatives. Rose Langwith is going to stay with me tonight. It isn't necessary, but Rose insisted."

She and Jim found themselves alone a few minutes later. He pulled her to him and gently cradled her head in his arms.

"I wish you'd let yourself go and cry," he whispered. "It might relieve you, darling. It frightens me to see you all tightened up like this."

"I don't feel like crying, Jim," she answered. "I want to keep going—help you all I can to square accounts for Dad."

"I'll square them—or die trying," was his grim response. "Nothing I can do will bring him back, but that bunch will pay a terrible price for what they've done." Jim's voice faltered. "You know what I thought of him; he was closer to me than my father. The day comes for every one of us when we've got to head for that ranch in the sky. I don't know what it's like, but I'm sure the Big Boss up there had the latchstring out for Kize."

Without the old man around the dingy sheriff's office wasn't the same. When Jim walked in that evening his eyes went to the battered desk where Kize had held forth for so many years. It brought a lump to his throat, and he was glad when Oats came in, for even in his most somber moments there was something tonic about the red-haired one.

"Well, we sure gave Kize a send-off such as Rock Crick never saw before." Oats declared proudly. "The old man would certainly have enjoyed it." He checked himself as he saw Jim's face grow long. "That won't help things a bit, Jim," he began again, unsmiling but not cast down. "We got to be thinkin' about the tomorrows if we're goin' to keep faith with him. Did

Corbett say anythin' about the slugs I took over?"

"He wants us to drop in tonight. You're sure you didn't get them mixed up?"

"Absolutely! I did exactly as he said. I heard that one of Mike Forney's horses had died. I went up to his place and began with the gun we took off of Ad Jenkins. I stood about thirty-five feet off and put a slug into the dead horse. I dug the slug out then and put it in an envelope and wrote on it what it was. I did the same with Silvey's gun next, and then with Kize's forty-five. There was no mixin' up about it."

"I just wanted to be sure," said Jim. "I'm counting on what Dan can make of them. We'll show up at his place a few minutes after eight."

The doctor was closeted with a patient when they arrived. After cooling their heels in the waiting-room for a quarter of an hour he joined them. Even before he spoke they knew he had good news.

"I've got something interesting for you," he told them. "Come on back to the laboratory; we won't be disturbed there."

On the bench where he worked they saw eight slugs lined up in a row, each resting on a piece of paper bearing words of identification.

"I want you to let me handle these things," Corbett told them. "They tell a story. You did a good job this afternoon, Oats; the slugs I got from you are flattened out just about as they'd be if they had been fired into human flesh. The scarifications are perfect."

"Go ahead," Jim urged. "Let's have it."

"All right. I'll begin with this one here. This is the slug I removed from Tom Yancey. And over here is one of the two I dug out of Jeff Foraker's chest. We know the first one was fired from Silvey's gun. This one here came from the same weapon. So he killed Yancey and shot Foraker."

"That's what we figured," Jim said. "You took two slugs out of Foraker. What about the other one?"

"This is it," Dan stated, touching another leaden pellet. "We don't have the gun that fired it. But—and get this—from that same gun came this slug and this one. The first is the bullet that killed Kize; the other is one that killed Chuck Silvey. One man murdered the two of them and helped to murder Foraker."

"Good grief!" Oats exploded. He sounded for all the world like old Kize. "You can state that for a fact, Doc?"

"I'm ready to put them under the microscope and prove it to you with your own eyes. And I can tell you that this slug over here, which is the one I removed at the autopsy on that Dutchman, Herman Ritter, who was killed and robbed two days before they got Foraker, came from that same gun. It means that whoever owns it has accounted for the lives of four men. I certainly believe if we had made autopsies in every case, we could charge other killings to him. Find him, Jim, and you've got either the ringleader of that gang or his first lieutenant."

"A forty-four, eh?" Jim queried tensely.

"A forty-four-caliber Colt, and I'd say from the sharpness of the scratches an eight-inch barrel. I don't think there's any question but it's an old Frontier Model single-action gun. There's a lot of them around, so that doesn't tell you too much."

"It tells me a lot. We know now that the evidence we found at the Hole the morning after Kize was killed wasn't misleading. You hit the nail on the head when you said Silvey had been killed somewhere else and the body just dumped there near Kize."

"I couldn't be mistaken about that, considering how little blood we found on the ground. Do you want to take charge of these slugs?"

Jim said no. "Take good care of them. They'll be just as safe with you as with me."

Corbett put them away carefully, first wrapping each one in the paper on which it stood.

"We can go back to my office," he suggested. "We'll be more comfortable there."

He led them in. Oats built himself a cigarette. They had talked for a quarter of an hour when a lull came in the conversation. Dan glanced at Jim. "I wonder," he said, "if the thought that's plaguing me has crossed your mind."

"What thought?" Jim asked.

"That the silver-handled gun that Wild Bill packs is a forty-four-caliber Frontier Model Colt."

"It's not Mullhall," Jim said positively. "He came along that afternoon when we were in the Blue Meadows investigating Jenkins's attempted stick-up of Rawhide Smith. Bill stuck around until just before we left. That rules him out."

"I don't know why, but I'm glad to hear it," Dan declared. "I know his record's bad and that he's a wild man when he's drunk. Maybe it's because I seem to see some good qualities in him. I was sorry to see Iris write that editorial."

"That won't happen again," said Jim. "Kize always felt that Bill was a sort of check on the gang that got him—that he was important to us. I know he was right. Morgan fears him. That's why he bought the *Enterprise*. He figures he can whip Iris into line and make her go after Mullhall tooth and nail. From what I told you I thought you guessed as much."

"I did," Dan acknowledged. "It's too bad you can't use Bill Mullhall."

"You mean, talk him into throwing in with the law?" Jim laughed skeptically. "I'm afraid not; Bill isn't built that way. If he was still the man he was when he was cleaning house for Wells, Fargo there might be a chance. But he's going his own way now, and he isn't going to turn noble for the law. Right now I'm more interested in Bar 66 than in Mullhall. The two of us are going up there in the morning."

"You think it's safe?"

"For a few days it will be. They've just killed one sheriff, Dan; they won't try to rub out another till things have quieted down."

Shep Failes, the coroner, had held an inquest in Dinwiddie's Hole the morning following the discovery of the two bodies. Duke Legrand, Morgan's foreman, was present and had been questioned at length. He disclaimed any knowledge of what had taken place. He had found Silvey's horse grazing along the south fork just after dawn. Chuck had been at the ranch, he said, and had left for town by way of the Squaw Hills. He didn't know what he was doing in Dinwiddie's Hole.

He was a rather tall hatchet-faced man of French extraction, nearing forty. His thin upper lip had an unpleasant way of lifting to expose his blackened silver bridgework. Jim and Oats had found him a dark, obscure individual whose thinly veiled hostility made him more suspect than ever in their eyes.

Oats spoke up. "If we go up through the Squaw Hills Legrand will figure we're still tryin' to get a lead on what happened at the Hole. We won't get anythin' out of him, but he may let somethin' else slip. If we don't accomplish anythin' else we can at least size things up." He glanced at Jim. "You goin' to give him the kid-glove treatment again?"

"Not particularly. If he gets tough we'll get tough with him."

They got away from town before nine next morning and were in sight of the Bar 66 house an hour and a half later.

They watched it for a time from a screening of trees.

"Looks peaceful enough," said Jim. There was some activity around the house and in the ranch yard. Along the creek bottom a small herd of cattle grazed contentedly.

"Yeh, but no work bein' done," Oats commented. "I figure work ain't what that bunch is here to do. Shall we ride in?"

"Might as well," Jim answered quietly. "Keep your eyes open. If you have to go for your gun, be quick about it. We'll have three or four to one against us."

Oats grinned recklessly. "I'll keep that in mind. I aim to go on livin' for years and years."

Chapter Ten

THE MISSING SLUG

Steve Gore, the only man of the Bar 66 crew who had worked on the Rock Creek range prior to catching on with Morgan's outfit, burst into the kitchen, where Legrand sat at the table drinking a cup of coffee. As Oats Ollinger had said, Steve Gore's reputation was bad; he had been suspected of rustling and stealing horses on several occasions and had once stood trial on the latter charge, only to have the case thrown out of court for lack of evidence.

"The law's payin' us a visit," he jerked out uneasily. "Lord and Ollinger are ridin' across the flats now."

"Is that so?" Legrand sneered. "I been expectin' 'em. I'll do the talkin', Steve. You stick around and tell the rest of the boys to do the same and make a bluff at being busy."

He finished his coffee before he got up. His gun belt hung from the back of a chair. He strapped it on and half pulled the gun from the holster, making sure it was free.

Steve had hurried out. When Legrand sauntered to the door the former was halfway down to the barn. There was no separate bunkhouse at Bar 66; just the main house, a barn, and several corrals. Jim and Oats were only two hundred yards away, moving at a comfortable, unhurried jog. The satisfied look on the foreman's sharp-featured face said he was confident he could handle them.

The visitors rode into the yard. Legrand continued to lounge in the open kitchen doorway, one hand pressed against the opposite side of the door frame to steady himself, a cigarette held lightly between his thin lips. He stood that way until they rode up to the door.

"Hi," Jim called out in impersonal greeting.

Legrand jerked a short nod and said, "Light."

They put their horses up to the rack and got down.

"We want to ask you a few questions," Jim told him.

Legrand nodded again. "You want to come in and take a load off your feet?"

They accepted his invitation and followed him into the kitchen, the sand on the unswept floor grating between their boots. In their time they had seen many ranch kitchens as well as houses, but never one on which so little money had been spent as this. A crude homemade table at which the whole crew ate stood in the center of the room. Only two or three battered chairs were in evidence. Upturned wooden boxes served for the rest. The stove was dirty with grease drippings and clogged with wood ashes. A cupboard that had been knocked together out of several packing-cases completed the furnishings. A pane of glass was missing from one of the windows. A board had been nailed over the opening.

Jim drew up a chair and sat down facing the foreman across the table. "We had another look at the Hole this morning," he said. "The couple times we've been up we noticed that your stock never drifts over that way."

"Not often," Legrand agreed. "Better graze along the crick; that keeps 'em from strayin'. Bein' cows, they don't like the lava they'd have to cross to get into the Hole."

"There's some droppin's—not too old—and a mess of cow tracks in there," Oats remarked. "I suppose you noticed?"

"No," Legrand muttered. He lit a fresh cigarette. He smoked tailored cigarettes. He tossed the pack on the table for them to help themselves. Oats took one. A shadow had fallen across the door. It was Steve Gore. He sat down on the step, apparently oblivious to what went on inside.

"I ain't been down there more'n once or twice since I caught on here," Legrand went on. "I was down the other day, of course, when you fellas was up with the coroner. As I remember it, the Hole would be a good place for a couple fellas to hold some of this stuff that they say is bein' rustled."

"That's the way it struck us," said Jim, anxious to proceed with this deception. "Tell me about Silvey. Or maybe you don't feel like talking; he and the boss were rather friendly."

"Go ahead," was the foreman's unperturbed response.

"He was often here, wasn't he?"

"Yeh, he was. Always in time for a free meal. He never hung around long."

"He always came alone?" Oats spoke up.

"Yeh. Oh, he may have had someone with him once or twice, but he was usually alone."

"I don't suppose he ever told you what the business was that brought him up this way so often?" Jim inquired.

"Sure! He was always on his way back to town from the Bend and was takin' the short cut down through the Squaw Hills. I swallowed it. Why should I question it?"

Lord shrugged. "I see what you mean." He felt that Duke Legrand's affability had a purpose, that he wanted to be drawn out about Chuck Silvey. It was not difficult to fathom, as the new sheriff saw it.

"When he pulled out he rode west, and I reckon you figured he was just going down the hills to town," Oats observed. He was taking his cues like an expert.

"Naturally!" Legrand exclaimed. "It never struck me that he was goin' to the Hole."

141

Jim sat up, pretending to be surprised. "You state that as a fact. Do you know he was bound for Dinwiddie's Hole?"

Legrand pushed his hat back from his forehead and laughed mirthlessly. "Suppose we quit kiddin' ourselves," he said thinly. "You know what I think, and I know what you think. Let's put the cards on the table. Chuck saw his chance—everybody hollerin' for beef and the price goin' sky-high. He got a couple boys together and set himself up in business. Can there be any question about it?"

Jim knew this was what the man had been leading up to from the first. The gang had killed Chuck because they knew he was suspect, rigged the killing of Kize on him, or so they believed, and were now ready to charge him with the rustling.

"I don't know," Jim declared thoughtfully. "If they slaughtered cattle in the Hole there ought to be some sign of the offal."

"Huh!" Legrand brushed that contention aside as worthless. "The coyotes and wildcats would make off with that in a hurry."

"They wouldn't make off with wagon tracks. If beef was slaughtered in the Hole, the meat had to be got out. There isn't a sign of a wagon track."

For a moment Jim and Oats thought they had Legrand trapped, but he slipped out of that tight corner without too much trouble.

"They could have packed the stuff out on horseback and had a wagon waitin' over on the Cabin Crick Road," he said.

"That's true," Jim agreed. "They could have gone out below the creek, and you would never have known anything about it." He secretly wondered if he was not making himself out too stupid to pass muster with Legrand.

But apparently not, for the latter said, "Naturally! I got a ranch to run; I don't give a damn about what the other fella's doin'. With Chuck under the ground, I reckon you won't hear about no more rustlin' for a spell. When a gang loses the boss it takes 'em some time to get reorganized."

Jim and Oats felt that this was a subject on which Duke could speak with authority. They sat there for another ten minutes or more, sizing up their man and the place. Through the window they could see half a dozen men loitering about the yard, several putting a new board into a damaged wagon box and the rest making a show of applying themselves to various tasks. Steve Gore continued to sit on the doorstep.

Legrand made no attempt to hurry his visitors on their way. He was well satisfied with what he believed he had accomplished. Across the table Jim and Oats also felt well repaid for their visit. They knew Legrand was shrewd, cunning, and as dangerous as a rattler. They also knew why Steve Gore had planted himself on the doorstep and why the rest of the crew remained in the yard.

The gun Duke was wearing was a Frontier Model Colt, its caliber a question, though it could hardly be other than a .44 or .45. It raised a question in Jim Lord's mind and in Oats's that kept recurring. Was this the gun that had killed old Kize?

"You been slaughtering any beef?" Jim asked.

Legrand said no. "Con sent up word a couple of days ago that he had enough to last a week or two. You know about the argument he had with Farraday over the ordinance."

The two men nodded.

"Where you been doin' your slaughterin'?" Oats inquired.

"In the barn," was the easy answer. "If you fellas want to have a look at it I'll take you back. You won't find any hides, if that's what you got on your mind. Mike Forney was up the other day and bought a wagonload of 'em. You want to go back?"

"I wouldn't mind," Jim told him.

Gore got up and let them pass. He and Oats exchanged a brief nod of recognition.

"You got a big crew for a spread this size, Duke," said Jim.

"Too big. But if Con don't mind payin' the wages it's none of my business. I reckon he's doin' well enough not to have to count the pennies."

It was an ingenious, disarming answer, quite in

keeping with everything Legrand had to say. It made the sheriff and Oats realize that they weren't dealing with any Chuck Silvey.

The south fork described a half circle just behind the barn, swinging within a few yards of it at one point. As they walked down the yard Jim saw a wildcat run out of the brush along the creek. He called the attention of the others to it and, whipping up his gun, fired at the animal. It was not a difficult shot. If he registered a clean miss it was because he hoped that Legrand would not lose an opportunity to show him up. He read the man correctly, for the foreman drew and fired in one motion, and the wildcat bounced into the air, a curled-up bundle of fur, and was dead when it struck the earth.

"Nice shooting!" Jim complimented Legrand. "I was way off."

He had accomplished his purpose; the gun was a .44. Oats thought to do even better. They walked over to where the animal lay. He turned it over with his boot.

"A big one," he commented. "Make a nice pair of mittens. You want that pelt particularly, Legrand?"

"No, go ahead, take it."

He called Steve over.

"You're handy with a skinnin' knife," he said. "Ollinger wants that pelt. Give him a hand with it."

He and Jim stood watching as Oats and Gore kneeled down and went to work. The pelt was soon jerked off. Oats turned the carcass over. The slug had gone almost through the animal. He could feel it just below the skin. Without any attempt at concealment he started to dig it out. Jim realized his purpose and felt his blood freeze. He couldn't say anything; he could only ask himself how Legrand could fail to sense why they were interested in examining the bullet.

Oats got the slug out and wiped it off. "Must have split that cat's heart," he declared. "Ain't flattened out a bit."

It was his intention to drop it into his pocket casually, but Legrand reached out for it. Oats had to pass it over.

"Never struck a rib or nothin'," Duke muttered, looking the pellet over with slight interest. "That don't happen very often." Done with it, he carelessly tossed the slug into the creek.

All Oats could do was to roll up the pelt and snarl to himself. Jim was even harder put to dissemble his disappointment and relief.

They found nothing in the barn to call for a question. Oats found a piece of cord, tied the unwanted pelt into a bundle, and then the three of them walked back to the horse rack beside the kitchen door.

"Duke, I want to thank you for the help you've given us about Silvey," Jim said before he swung up into the saddle. "You don't get to town often, do you?"

"No, I stick purty close to home. I get over to the store at Spanish Ford now and then."

"That's where we're heading now. You found a short cut?"

"You can go over that ridge and drop down into the Blue Meadows." Legrand realized as soon as the words left his lips that he had made a slip. "That's what the boys tell me," he ran on quickly. "Personally, I'm never in too big a hurry to go around by way of the road. Why punish a horse?"

Steve Gore overheard him and had to turn away to conceal his amused amazement. That was good—Duke having mercy on a bronc!

Jim was equally undeceived, but he said, "That's right. I reckon we'll take the road; the day's still young."

They rode off without glancing back, their silence holding until the Bar 66 house was far behind them.

"Well," Jim muttered, "you can blow off now if you want to."

"Good Christopher! That close to it and have him throw that slug in the crick!"

"I'll say you were close to it!" Jim rapped out angrily. "You came within an inch of tipping him off to what you were after! Let him get the idea that we're matching slugs and he'll get rid of that gun in a hurry!"

"Oh, I coulda covered myself," Oats protested, aggrieved. "I'd have said somethin' to throw him off the scent. I knew I was on thin ice, but there it was, and I figured I could take a chance."

"Grow up!" Jim snapped. "You take any chances with that gent and you'll find yourself in Phelan's funeral parlor. He's just plain poison, and don't you make any mistake about it!"

"He ain't so Godawful smart," Oats argued. "He slipped up there at the last second."

"And he knew it. Now we've got this long ride for nothing. I bet that gang has worn a trail across the ridge into the Meadows."

"We can lay out there," Oats offered.

Jim shook his head. "Too late for that. Legrand made a slip. It'll scare him off; he won't take a chance on having fooled us. You won't hear of any more robberies there. We can begin looking somewhere else."

Chapter Eleven

SUSPICIOUS ACCIDENT

Coming down the slope at Spanish Ford, the sheriff and Oats had a bird's-eye view of the diggings. It was noon, but no one seemed to have knocked off working.

"Busy as a bunch of ants," Oats remarked. "Reckon not many of 'em are doin' as well as old Rawhide."

"He was lucky," said Jim. "He came late, got his in a hurry, and had the good sense to call it a day. There's more tents far up the Bend than there was last week. You know what that means?"

"Sure. Old claims peterin' out and men tryin' new gravel. I don't know why those bars shouldn't be as rich as the ones down here."

Jim shrugged. "I couldn't tell you one way or the other. But the creek was prospected as far as the portal a week or ten days after the rush started. All anyone found up there was a color. I'm afraid this camp will be good only as long as the lower bars continue to produce."

They found Johnnie Montero doing his usual thriving business. The platform or stoop in front of the store was piled high with merchandise that had been delivered that morning but which Johnnie and his clerks had been too busy to wheel inside.

Through a window Jim and Oats saw Little Ben Riley in his cubicle sorting mail. He bore no marks of the beating he had received from Wild Bill. They left their horses at the rack and walked in. Johnnie called a greeting but was too busy to talk with them for a few minutes. They went to the rear and sat down. When the Basque was free he joined them. He spoke of Kize and expressed his regrets at the old man's death.

"Johnnie, let's have some cheese and crackers and a can of sardines," Oats interjected.

"No," Johnnie protested. "Maria call down in couple minute. You fella come upstair and have dinner with me." He raised his head, sniffed the mingled fragrance of garlic and some savory nutlike aroma drifting down from above, and grinned. "That's *garbanzos* and some Basco sausage. You like heem, all right! That Maria, she's damn good cook."

They accepted his hospitality with alacrity. As they waited to be called Jim said, "I've never seen the store busier, Johnnie."

"Yeh, she's good—so long as she last." The Basque's tone was skeptical.

"What do you mean?" Jim asked.

"Another bad week along the creek. That's two in row. Some fella go way up by the portal. Don't find not'ing. I know what that mean. You see. Theece week plenty fella leave camp. Three, four go theece morning. Next week mebbe they leave by hundred."

The few mining experts who had examined the Rustlers' Bend diggings had said without exception that the camp was not a permanent one, that the gravel would be exhausted in a year at most. Recent indications had led Jim to believe that even that estimate was overly optimistic, but he had had no idea that the end was already in sight. If true, he had little time left in which to track down the bandit gang that had capped its long list of crimes with the killing of Kize Farraday.

"Johnnie, is it really as bad as that?" he asked, not trying to hide his concern.

"Oh, I talk beeg weeth the boys. Say mebbe next week she be a beeg one again. But I don't geeve no more credit. She's cash from now on. When theece theeng blow up I don't want her to blow up in my face."

His wife called, and they went upstairs to dinner. An hour later they were on their way to town. Jim had little to say. Oats knew what was on his partner's mind.

"Don't let it get you down," the red-haired man chirped. "We've got a couple weeks or more. That'll be time enough."

"We can't count on having two or three weeks.

151

When the camp begins to fade, the first ones to leave this country will be the birds we want. It was always Kize's idea, and it's been mine, that we could work things up to a showdown that would blow the lid off of everything. We're not ready for it; we haven't evidence enough. But if we wait we may lose them. I'm going to give it some thought, I promise you. I'll do something in a day or two."

A plan of action occurred to him before the afternoon was over. His first inclination was to dismiss it as harebrained and utterly absurd. And yet the more thought he gave it, the less preposterous it seemed. He knew Kize would have vetoed it instantly. It meant risking everything on a long gamble whose chief virtue was its audacity.

"I better forget it," he decided. That evening, however, he found himself discussing it with Iris. She was anything but enthusiastic.

"It's too wild, isn't it?" he queried.

"It's not only that, Jim; I don't know whether I could get away with my part of it. Morgan never comes to the office, but I'm sure one of the boys in the pressroom is spying for him."

"Say that you could do it—and I'd see that you were well protected—what would you think about it?"

Iris shook her head. "I don't know," she said thoughtfully. "I don't want you to pin me down;

you've certainly got two or three days to think it over. I'd like to discuss it with Dan; he has a good head for such things. And you know, of course, that almost the first thing you'd have to do would be to sell the idea to Otis Longyear."

"I suppose so!" Jim muttered disgustedly. "That would be the end of it. I'll have to come up with something else."

Jim did not stay late. Iris had put in a full day at the *Enterprise*. But, though she was tired, he was glad to see that some of the tightness had left her face. She walked to the gate with him, and when he kissed her good night she clung to him, and a sob shook her.

"Thank God I've got you," she whispered. "I don't know what I'd do without you, Jim. They could kill you too—I know. I hope Rustlers' Bend becomes a ghost camp, and soon. Anything to end this nightmare."

"It'll be over soon enough," he assured her. "Rock Creek will be just the quiet little cow town it used to be. Nobody will get rich, but there'll be a good living for all."

"I'll like it better that way. I wonder what will become of the *Enterprise*? It wouldn't pay to publish it daily."

"No," he agreed. "Hustis got out at the right time. After Morgan is washed out of the picture and the boom days are over the paper will go to someone for a song."

"I'd love to have the *Enterprise* for my own," Iris declared, her voice rising with eagerness. "I've made it a good newspaper that's respected all over Nevada. I couldn't bear to see it go back to what it was when I took over."

"Well, we'll see," Jim said encouragingly. "Maybe we can arrange it."

The following day was to prove that coming events do not always cast their shadow before them. The morning wore on peacefully in Rock Creek, but between town and the Bend events were taking place that were destined to set the stage for the violence that was to follow.

Three miles below Spanish Ford, Misery Creek, which was actually the north fork of Rock Creek, cut across the road that served the diggings. For ten months a year it was a meandering, slow-flowing little rivulet. During the spring runoff, however, it brought down an icy torrent from the slope of distant Mount Misery, where it headed. As a result, the creek bed was badly eroded. Where it cut the Rustlers' Bend Road the banks were ten feet deep, necessitating the construction of one of the first bridges built in the county. Soon after the rush had got under way the county's road superintendent had replaced many of the old timbers with new ones and pronounced it safe for the heaviest loads.

For several months it had stood up under the

154

test of Bill Mullhall's freighting-outfits. This morning, however, it had given way as one of his twelve-mule teams and a string of wagons was crossing. It had plunged to the bottom, carrying two wagons with it, injuring a driver and several animals, and spilling the contents of the wagons—mostly flour and canned goods—into the creek.

Mullhall's ranch was less than three miles up Misery Creek. Word was sent to him at once. In the meantime traffic began to pile up at the wrecked bridge; it was impossible for the stages, as well as anything else that rolled on wheels, to get through.

Word of the accident reached town promptly, and Jim and Oats set out for the scene at once. When they arrived they found Wild Bill there and in a towering rage. The injured mules had been put out of their agony. Bill's men were making an effort to snake the wrecked wagons back on the road. He was down under the bridge, examining the approaches and turning the air blue with his violent profanity.

The sheriff and Oats made a rapid calculation of the damage.

"It'll cost him a couple thousand dollars," the red-haired man declared. "Three mules shot, a couple of wagons smashed up, and the goods that's spoiled. He's responsible for 'em, I reckon."

"Let's get down and talk to him," said Jim. "He's blowing off like a wild man."

Bill turned on them wolfishly, his pocked face lined with wrath. Jim started to say something about it being a bad accident. He didn't get far.

"Accident, hell!" Mullhall roared. "This was no accident! The bridge was tampered with! It was aimed at me! I'm the only one who's puttin' heavy loads over it!"

"You mean the timbers were cut and the bridge left hanging?" Jim demanded.

"Hell, no! That would have been too much of a giveaway! Look under there! The approaches was undermined! It's the same on the other side!"

There was some evidence that the ground had been cut away.

"A freshet could have done it," Jim pointed out.

"Don't tell me anythin' like that!" Bill yelped. "That was picks and shovels! I know who did it! By God, they'll pay for it!"

"You better take it easy, Bill, and be sure before you fly off the handle," Jim advised.

"I'll make sure it was no accident! I guarantee you I'll make sure!"

Oats spoke up. "The first thing for you to do is get your stages runnin'. They can get through by way of the Idaho Road and come down through your ranch."

"I ain't interested in gettin' 'em through! They

can stand where they are and rot till I get the low-down on this deal!"

Mullhall climbed out of the creek bottom and harangued one of his men, Cass Curry, for several minutes, ordering him to salvage what they could of the flour and canned stuff. He swung into the saddle then and raced away in the direction of his ranch. Stopping at the house only long enough to arm himself with a sixteen-foot stock whip, Wild Bill took off for Spanish Ford, riding like a man possessed.

Jim and Oats watched the salvaging operations for a few minutes. Both were asking themselves where Mullhall was bound.

"Are we goin' to stick around here?" Oats inquired, a frown puckering his young face.

"We better wait until Blenis and his road crew show up," Jim answered. "They know about the bridge by now; they'll be here directly."

"You figure the bridge was tampered with?"

Jim nodded. "I'm afraid it was. Something bothering you?"

"Bill. He said he was goin' to find out what was what. He ain't goin' into town. I don't believe he's headin' for Bar 66. That leaves only one place."

"Spanish Ford?"

"Yeh. Jim, if this was a job, Little Ben Riley knows about it. He had somethin' to square with Bill. There'll be hell to pay when they come together. Bill will get the truth out of him or kill him. If we stick around here much longer we'll be too late."

"You're right!" Lord agreed, reversing himself on the instant. "We can put our broncs across the creek most any place. Let's be moving!"

Chapter Twelve

A GROWLING, ANGRY MOB

With their first glimpse of Spanish Ford they saw a crowd of fully one hundred men gathered in front of Montero's store. It was a growling, angry crowd. When they rode up they understood the reason. Wild Bill had Little Ben roped to the hitchrack and was cutting him to ribbons with the stock whip. Every time the leaden popper struck it plucked out a piece of the cripple's shirt and slashed his flesh. The front of him was already a bloody mess.

Mullhall was an artist with the stock whip. He could call his shots, and when he took aim the deadly popper found its mark.

"Stop him!" someone in the crowd yelled. "He'll kill Little Ben!"

Others echoed the frantic cry, but the men from the diggings lacked a leader who could translate their horror and wrath into action. Big Johnnie Montero stood on the stoop imploring Wild Bill to desist. Now for the first time the latter fixed his attention on him, and it was lethal in its intensity.

"Keep your lip buttoned, you big grease ball, or

159

you'll get some of the same! I ain't askin' him who done it—if the bridge was wrecked, I know who done it! All he's got to tell me is, was a job done on it! He knows, the little rat!"

"But you'll keel him, Bill!"

"You're damned right I'll kill him if he don't talk!"

The stiffness had gone out of Little Ben. His head lolled on his chest, and only the rope that bound him held him erect.

"He's out on his feet, unconscious!" a bearded miner cried in violent protest. "Shame on you, Mullhall! Don't hit the little fella with the whip again!"

The crowd rallied behind that cry, and its anger swelled to a menacing roar. Beside himself though he was, a warning was telegraphed to Wild Bill's brain. He half swung around and faced the men. One look at those grim faces and he knew that the strange inexplicable alchemy that transforms an angry crowd into a savage mob had taken place. Though realizing that his situation was suddenly desperate, he refused to back away. He saw the crowd edge forward a step and stand there poised to rush in at him, when Jim and Oats broke through, their guns leveled.

"That's far enough!" Jim rapped. "We're taking charge here!"

There was something in the dead-level quality of his voice that carried conviction. He whipped off his hat and tossed it at the feet of the men in the front row.

"That hat's the deadline," he told them. "We'll shoot the man that crosses it." To Oats he whispered, "You hold them! I'll take care of Mullhall."

He fell back to where Wild Bill stood, the whip in one hand, the other on his gun. Beads of perspiration stood out on Mullhall's broad face.

"You went too far this time, Bill," Jim told him. "You're under arrest, but I'm going to let you go on your own recognizance. I'll find you when I want you. You fork your bronc now and get out of here."

A snarling grunt was the only sound that came from Wild Bill's lips. He had a reputation to maintain, and, exhibitionist that he was, he coolly coiled his stock whip, knotted the popper, and ran his arm through the loop until he had the whip draped over his shoulder. Giving his gun belt a hitch, he swaggered over to his horse, his round ferretlike eyes burning feverishly. He was an excellent horseman, and he swung into the saddle with a flourish. As soon as he was seated he raked the bronc with the spurs and with a wild yell drove through the crowd at a slashing gallop, scattering men right and left.

Many of them were armed. It would have been a simple matter to send a fusillade of shots in Mullhall's direction, even as some of them had fired on another occasion at Chuck Silvey. For Mullhall to have escaped unmarked would have been a minor miracle. That not a hand was raised to stop him was due solely to the coolness and determination of the sheriff and Ollinger.

Jim realized that the situation was still ticklish. Proof of it came almost at once, and the anger of the crowd was now directed at him.

"If you think you saved his rotten hide you're mistaken, Mr. Sheriff!" It was the tall bearded man who had spoken his mind to Wild Bill. "We know where to find him as well as you! There'll be more to this, I'm telling you!"

There was a chorus of approval from the crowd. Montero had slashed the rope that bound Little Ben and placed him on the stoop.

"Break it up, boys," Jim ordered. "A couple of you give Johnnie a hand and carry Riley to his tent. I'll send to town for the doctor." He walked over to recover his hat, and the men fell back before him.

The crowd disintegrated slowly. When he considered it safe Jim had a look at Little Ben, who had recovered consciousness. At Jim's shoulder Oats muttered, "Looks like he'd been put through a meat grinder."

Someone got a blanket. Little Ben was placed on it and carried to his tent. Montero came out after a few minutes, shaking his head as he joined Jim and Oats.

"I'll feex up some of the small cut weeth sheep dip," Johnnie told them. "Corbett will have to sew up the beeg cuts. You better tell him to come queeck."

"All right, Oats," said Jim, "you get started. Go over the ridge to Bar 66 and down through the Squaw Hills. Bring Dan back that way. If you ride out in the open you shouldn't run into trouble. I'll wait here."

Oats got away at once, and Jim walked into the store with Johnnie. The barrel-chested Basque continued to pour out a bilingual denunciation of Wild Bill.

"Somet'ing should be done weeth that fella, and I don't mean just lock him up," he growled. "*Por Dios*, I t'ink mebbe MacHugh is right; theece is not the end of it."

"MacHugh is the tall gent with the beard?" Jim asked.

"*Si*. Andy MacHugh. He's good man, but theece too much for heem. The word go up the creek today. Mebbe tonight couple hundred of the boys go on Mullhall's place and streeng him up. Mebbe you don't stop 'em next time."

"They'll cool off during the day." Jim wasn't as sure about it in his mind as he sounded.

Oats arrived with Corbett shortly after noon.

"You got here sooner than I expected," Jim told them. "You must have had clear sailing, Oats."

"Yeh, didn't see a soul."

Dan went into the tent where Little Ben lay and was busy with him for the better part of an hour. Jim and Oats sat on the stoop in front of Montero's store.

"How did things go up here?" Oats inquired. Jim shook his head.

"I don't know. I didn't have any trouble. The men went back to their claims, but they didn't go to work. They stood around in groups of five to ten talking up something. Look up the Bend; you can see them doing it right now. I don't like it. Johnnie thinks they may go after Mullhall tonight."

"It wouldn't surprise me," Oats declared soberly. "God knows he's asked for it. We goin' to stick around?"

"No, we'll go back with Dan, but only as far as Misery. We'll put in the rest of the day there. After dark we'll cut across country and camp out on the Idaho Road. I'm not going to have Mullhall lynched if I can prevent it. Don't say anything to Dan about this. It'd get back to Iris. She's got enough on her mind."

Corbett pronounced Little Ben's condition serious due to the loss of blood. Some of the cuts were deep, and he predicted that the man's recovery would be slow and painful. After leaving some instructions with Johnnie he left with Jim and Oats.

Within a mile of the Ford they met a stage. Jim

stopped it and was told that Cass Curry, the man Wild Bill had left in charge at the creek, was transferring passengers, mail, and express at the bridge and having the north and southbound stages turn around.

"Is Cal Blenis on the job?" Jim inquired of the driver.

"Yeh, he's there with a road crew clearin' things away."

The stage rolled on.

At the crossing Jim found a line of ranch wagons laden with supplies lined up below the wrecked bridge. Strung out behind them were three or four buckboards.

"I don't know what they're waitin' for," said Oats. "They won't get across here for a couple days."

Jim got Blenis aside and asked his opinion on why the bridge had caved in.

"The rock underpinning was removed," the road superintendent told him. "I built this bridge. We placed some boulders and set the timbers on 'em. I examined the bridge only a couple weeks ago. It was as sound as a dollar. Musta taken three or four men all night to dig the boulders out and roll 'em into the creek. They filled the holes with loose earth and just left the stringers hanging there. It was sure to go down with the first heavy load that was put on it."

"Then Bill was right."

"He sure was! The dirty skunks was out to get him, and no mistake. I ain't trying to tell you how to handle your job, Lord, but destroying a bridge is a crime. It's up to you to find out who they was."

Jim nodded without taking offense and said, "That's my job. I'll take care of it, Cal. Why are all those wagons and rigs lining up over there? You got any hope of getting them across by night-fall?"

"The light ones. I got some new timbers coming up. I'll drop a couple in place and lay some loose planks on 'em. Be a week before the stages and Bill's freighters can get across."

Corbett continued on to town after a few minutes. For the rest of the afternoon Jim and Oats whiled away their time at the bridge, being met on every hand by the same question—who was out to get Mullhall? Their only answer was that they didn't know. It was received with a shaking of heads and rising doubts as to their fitness for the jobs they held.

"They don't think much of us, Oats," Jim remarked with a thin smile.

"If we could tell 'em half what we know they'd change their tune."

The new timbers arrived. By six o'clock several were in place. Planks salvaged from the old bridge were laid on them. Presently the ranch wagons and lighter vehicles were led across the temporary structure. A watchman, who was to remain on duty through the night, began lighting and placing a number of red lanterns.

"Where do we find our supper?" Oats asked when he saw Blenis and his crew leaving for town.

"I guess we don't," Jim replied. "We can get away from here anytime now. Pull up your belt a notch, and we'll ride."

When Jim was mounted he rode up the road to where Cass Curry stood talking with Mullhall's skinners. "Curry, you sticking it out here tonight?"

"That seems to be the idea. Bill said the wagons was to stand right where they are, so they stand here till he tells me to get 'em rollin'."

"You know that he got in a bit over his head at the Ford, don't you?" Jim asked.

Curry nodded. "Frank Woodmancy told me when he came down on the afternoon stage."

"Maybe it would be a good idea if you rode up to the ranch this evening and got some new instructions," Jim advised. "It's just possible you might be more use to him up there than here."

Curry's eyes narrowed as he looked up at him. There was tough fiber in him, and it was reflected in his hard-bitten face. "I'm much obliged for the tip," he muttered. "But Frank said he'd get word to me if them gravel scratchers along the Bend was crazy enough to go out to get Bill this evenin'."

"Okay," Jim told him. "Woodmancy's got another guard and a driver up there with him. That adds up to only three men. If any real trouble blows up they won't be given a chance to get word to anyone; they'll be rounded up right off the bat. But you do as you please."

He swung his horse and rode off with Oats at his side. Two miles above the road they forded Misery Creek and after striking through a fringe of low hills came in sight of the Idaho Road.

"Better pull up, eh?" Oats queried. Jim nodded.

"It's a good spot. We'll leave the broncs here and go up to the top of this knoll. There won't be any moon tonight until late. We'll have to depend on the stars."

"And our ears," Oats added. "If a mob starts over from the Ford we'll hear 'em long before we see 'em."

Even in the gathering twilight a considerable stretch of the road was visible from the crest of the knoll. They looked it over carefully. It was still so early that they pulled off their boots and relaxed on the ground. Oats soon fell asleep and snored loudly. Black night had fallen when he roused himself.

"What time is it?" he asked.

"A few minutes after eight. Don't light that cigarette. We may not be alone around here."

"What makes you say that?" Oats demanded, blinking owlishly.

"Well, I figure a mob isn't likely to hoof it all the way from the Ford unless they know for sure that Mullhall's at the ranch. The most likely thing for them to have done was to send someone over this afternoon to keep cases on him."

Several minutes passed before Oats said, "You sound purty sure that we're goin' to have our hands full."

"No," Jim demurred, "I'm anything but sure. I'm not hunting trouble. We made that crowd toe the line this morning, but it'll be a different story tonight. They won't be backed down so easily a second time."

"Reckon not. If they get this far they'll be steamed up proper. What are you goin' to do if they show up—light out for Mullhall's ranch and fort up there with him and his men?"

"The first thing to do will be to warn him what's up. As for the rest of it, I'll cross that bridge when I get to it. If you don't—"

"Listen!" Oats broke in. "Do you catch that?"

"Yeh! They're coming for sure!"

They listened, and the dull rumble of many voices, not unlike the breaking of surf on a sandy shore, grew with every passing second.

Jim got to his feet. Oats stood up beside him. Together they kept their eyes glued on the road. By the frosty light of the stars they saw the mob.

"Good Christopher!" came from Oats in a

smothered cry. "Must be two hundred of 'em!"

"Come on," Jim muttered. "Get mounted. If we hurry we can reach Bill's place half an hour ahead of them."

Chapter Thirteen

RIPE FOR LYNCHING

A man came out of the house when he heard Jim and Oats ride up to the hitchrack. "Well?" he growled before he recognized the sheriff and his deputy. "Oh, you," he added less belligerently.

"Bill here?" Jim demanded.

"Inside."

He opened the door and followed them into what had once been the parlor of the old house. A plain pine table long enough to accommodate a dozen men sat in the center of the room. Wild Bill sat there, a glass and bottle handy. Across the table from him Cass Curry was getting a dressing-down for leaving the bridge. Ranged around the room were seven others—shotgun guards, stage drivers, and two who did no known work, but lived on Mullhall's bounty.

"You get back to the wagons and stay there!" Bill railed at Curry. "When I want you here I'll tell you!"

He had been drinking. He wasn't drunk, but he was far enough along to be an unreasoning, snarling brute. Sight of Jim further infuriated him. He didn't ask the sheriff what he was doing there.

"You, eh!" he roared. "I tell this bastard to stay with the wagons; you tell him he's needed here! Who's givin' the orders to my men, Lord—you or me?"

"Shut up!" Jim rapped. "If you want to save your rotten neck you'll listen to me. You've got just thirty minutes to decide whether you want to be jerked to Jesus or make a run for it. There's a mob of two hundred men on their way over here from the Ford to string you up, and they mean business!"

It pulled Cass Curry and the others to rigid attention. Mullhall pushed back from the table and glared at Jim with menacing eyes.

"You're lyin'!" he snarled. "Those white-livered punks wouldn't have the guts to come after me!"

"Open the door and listen," Jim flung back. "You'll hear 'em. They'll be marching into the yard in half an hour."

It had a profound effect on Wild Bill. He shook his head as though to clear it of the alcoholic fumes that clouded his mind. He got to his feet. He didn't go to the door; something told him he didn't need the evidence of his ears.

"You mean it!" he acknowledged with a low growl. As he stood there breathing heavily his truculence and insufferable insolence ran out of him like sand from an overturned glass. When he spoke he was suddenly stone-sober. "I'm obliged to you, sheriff. I ain't runnin'. When they come through my gate that mob will meet gunfire."

"Use your brains, Bill," Jim advised grimly. "You can't kill two hundred men. Kill one or two, and nothing short of hell itself will stop the rest from getting you. I saved your hide this morning, and I'll do my best to save it again tonight; you're my prisoner, and it's my duty to protect you. You've got your choice; play it my way or go it alone."

"What do you mean, your way?"

"No gunplay, for one thing. I'll be at the gate, when they get here—just Oats and me. I don't want you or your men to show your faces. I'm not fool enough to think I can stop them by throwing any fear or respect for the law into them. There is only one thing I can say that'll have any effect on them—that's to tell 'em the truth about Little Ben Riley. It's the last thing in the world I want to do—it'll scramble all my plans—but my hand is being forced, and I'll have to lay it on the line."

"No!" Oats objected vehemently. "Why should you throw everythin' away to save this rough-neck's hide? Tell the mob that Riley's the informer for the gang, that it was him who put the finger on the men who was robbed and killed, and you'll start a blackleg stampede out of this country as soon as the word gets around!

173

You'll lose 'em all—even Little Ben. He'll be dragged out of bed and lynched before midnight!"

"I appreciate all that," Jim muttered grimly, "but it's the only thing I can do. If I move fast enough I may be able to grab off most of them." His attention flashed back to Wild Bill. "What do you say?"

"What the hell can I say but yes?" was the sullen response. "If you can turn 'em back at the gate, okay! But I ain't goin' to be caught in this house like a trapped rat! There's enough of us here to give a good account of ourselves. If I have to go under, I'm goin' down fightin'!"

Though he was alive to his danger and felt the cold fingers of fear gripping him, he tried to bluster his way out, ignoring his men and taking their loyalty for granted. One of them opened the door, and the angry roar of the approaching mob rolled into the room with a menacing rumble. The men shifted about nervously, and Bill's cheek muscles drooped.

"You better get down there, Lord," he muttered, his surliness gone. "If they'll listen to you, talk fast. Ask 'em why Riley always had so much to say to Chuck Silvey."

"I know what to say," Jim returned bluntly. "Put out the lamps. Come on, Oats; we'll leave our broncs at the rack and walk down to the gate. Be a few minutes before they show up."

They reached the ranch gate, a crude affair built of aspen saplings and barbed wire that could be flattened in a minute or two.

"That won't hold 'em back," Oats remarked solemnly. "You realize that we're going to find ourselves caught in the middle if your palaverin' doesn't work? Mullhall and his bunch will open up from the house, and this mob will let fly at us from the other direction."

"I know," Jim said quietly. "We'll have to keep a cool head. Don't make the mistake of reachin' for your gun; talk will have to turn the trick, or nothing will."

Before long they caught sight of the mob. Presently they could see bearded Andy MacHugh in the lead. Just behind him walked two men with coiled ropes over their shoulders.

"They'll see us directly," said Jim. "I'll hail MacHugh when he gets near enough so my voice will carry. That'll let him know who we are."

When he called out the men from the diggings were less than a hundred yards away. They recognized his voice.

"Come up to the gate, MacHugh; I've something to say to you!"

It brought an angry yell from the mob. "No sheriff's stoppin' us tonight!" one of them cried. "Tell him to get out of the way, Mac; we're goin' through!"

They came on until they were pressing against the flimsy gate.

"Can you speak for these men, MacHugh?" Jim demanded.

"That I can! You're wasting your time, Mr. Sheriff, if you think we'll be swayed by your gab. You saved Mullhall's bacon this morning. Don't think you can do it tonight."

"Maybe you'll feel different about it when I open your eyes to the truth." Jim spoke with an incisiveness that won him a hearing. "A dozen men from the diggings have been murdered in the past ten weeks. Twice that many or more have been slugged and robbed of their gold. And yet you're here tonight to avenge the wrongs of the double-crossing little rat who's had a finger in every killing and robbery that's been committed since you came to the Bend. I'm only saying what I've known for weeks. Kize Farraday knew it, too. Little Ben Riley is the informer for the gang that's responsible for the lawlessness that's left no man safe."

His startling accusation was met with cries of "Liar!" and hoots of derision. "Why didn't you arrest him if you knew he was a crook?" someone shouted.

"Yes, why didn't you?" MacHugh repeated.

"Because I thought that through him I could get the evidence I need to hang the actual killers and ringleaders. You've forced me to speak, even though it's likely to mean that they'll flee the country now."

He told them how Little Ben had used the forwarding-address dodge, how he had marked the wagons carrying gold. What he didn't know he let his imagination supply. He saw that he was convincing them, and he threw caution to the winds. He mentioned Mullhall and what Cal Blenis had told him about the Misery Creek Bridge.

"I don't owe Bill Mullhall a thing," he went on. "But I can tell you this—the bandit gang that's made every one of you wonder if you'd be the next man to be shot down fear him. Without Mullhall things would be worse than they are. He's in the house with a bunch of his men. They'll shoot it out with you. If you still think Bill Mullhall is the man you want, go get him."

With Oats he walked away from the gate and left them to their own decision. The crowd milled around for a few minutes, everybody talking at once. There were friends and acquaintances of Jeff Foraker, Dutch Ritter, Tom Yancey, and many of the other men who had died violently at the hands of the gang among them. They began whooping it up against Little Ben. They were for hurrying back to the Ford, questioning Riley, and, if he couldn't clear himself, stringing him up on the nearest tree.

Since all were bent on vengeance, it did not take them long to decide that Little Ben should pay for his treachery. Even those who, a few minutes ago, had been loudest in denouncing Wild Bill were forced to admit that their score against the postmaster at Spanish Ford was far heavier. Vowing that this night's work should not go for nothing, they began a disorderly return to the creek.

"Well, you had your way; you turned 'em back," Oats grumbled. "It's what you might call a dismal success, if you ask me. You didn't only expose your hand—you put a rope around Riley's neck for sure."

"We've got a few minutes to do something about that," Jim replied over his shoulder as he hurried back to the house.

Someone struck a light when he burst in. Mullhall kneeled at an open window, a rifle cradled in his arms.

"You won't need that," Jim said thinly.

"Reckon not," Bill answered, a new respect for Lord in his tone. "You did all right."

"I'm going to the Ford, and I aim to get there in a hurry," Jim told him. "I want Curry to go with us. You've got three men there. You send word by Curry that they're to do as I say; I want Ben Riley alive."

"You're crazy, Lord!" Mullhall protested. "You'll never get away with it!"

"I will if I hurry. We'll toss him into your stage, carry him across the temporary bridge at Misery, place him in one of your wagons, and have him behind bars by midnight."

"Okay," Bill agreed. "You tell the boys to do as the sheriff says, Curry."

Curry's bronc had been turned into the corral. He put a saddle on it quickly, and with Jim directing their course the three of them got away, skirting through to the south of the low hills until they were ahead of the mob. They cut into the Idaho Road then and reached the Ford with approximately half an hour to accomplish their purpose.

The deserted camp was still awake. Lights burned in Johnnie's store. From the tents along the creek came the shrill, hardened voices of the women, some raised in laughter and others in the usual bickering that went on endlessly there. Two miners sat on the stoop in front of Montero's place. They jumped to their feet when the sheriff's party pulled up sharply before the board-and-canvas office of the stage line next door. The miners were armed, and they didn't hold back even when they recognized Jim and his companions.

"Hey, wait a minit!" one of them challenged. "You can't go in there tonight!"

Oats had them covered in a second. "Drop your guns,' he snapped. "This is the law, and we'll go where we damned please!"

The miners gave in. The angry voices brought Montero to the door.

"Get inside, Johnnie, and keep out of this," Jim ordered. "Come on—be quick about it!"

Johnnie's discretion outweighed his curiosity. Growling to himself, he stepped back inside and slammed the door.

It was dark in the headquarters of the stage line. Curry struck a match. By its flickering light they saw three men on the floor, bound hand and foot.

"Just as I thought," said Jim. "They were taken by surprise and tied up before they could do anything about it."

"You said it!" Frank Woodmancy, who rode shotgun for Mullhall, exclaimed. "We was eatin' supper when they jumped us. Cut these ropes, Cass, and get us out of this fix."

Curry lighted a lantern first. He had the men freed from their bonds a moment or two later, but not without a raucous laugh at their expense.

"The boss says the three of you are to do whatever the sheriff tells you," he told them.

Woodmancy and the other two looked to Jim for their orders.

"You want to step lively," he said. "No time for explanations. Hitch the team and hook up as quickly as you can. Curry, you come with me. We'll snatch Riley out of his tent and put him in the stage. I want to be rolling away from the Ford in ten minutes at the latest."

Leaving Oats to guard the two miners, they crossed to Little Ben's tent. He lay on a canvas cot, sleeping fitfully. He heard them coming and was wide awake when they entered. "Who is it?" he asked.

"Sheriff," Jim answered tersely. "I'm taking you to town. Stop your yammering. If you take it easy we'll try not to hurt you."

The cripple started to protest. They shut him up and carried him in a blanket to the stage a hundred yards away. Woodmancy, the other guard, and the driver were already moving up from the corral in back with the harnessed team. Hooking up took only a minute or two.

Montero watched from inside his door. Others, possibly a score, looked on from a distance. Little Ben had been removed from his tent so quickly and quietly that they were not aware of it. But they knew, as every man within half a mile of Spanish Ford did, what the crowd that had left camp earlier in the evening had in mind and that as a preliminary Frank Woodmancy and the driver and other guard had been trussed up to prevent them from carrying a warning to Wild Bill. Obviously something had gone wrong, for here was the sheriff, as well as Woodmancy and Mullhall's other men, getting the stage ready to roll. That in itself puzzled them; heretofore no stage had ever left camp after nightfall.

Jim was aware of their hostile scrutiny. He was equally alive to the fact that their number was growing with every passing minute. With a smothered sigh of relief he heard Shorty Williams, the driver, say, "That does it! We can roll!"

"Climb aboard," Jim told him. "Don't waste any time about it. Curry, you ride on the box with him. Woodmancy, you and your partner get up on top."

He called to Oats. The two of them mounted. Shorty cracked his whip, and the six-horse team leaped away.

"Your luck is sure standin' up for you," Oats said, raising his voice to make himself heard above the rumbling of the wheels. "The rest ought to be easy."

Jim nodded. Little Ben was watching him intently. Finally the latter said, "Did they get Mullhall?"

"They did not. They're on their way back to camp to get you."

"Me?" Riley half raised himself from the seat where he lay.

"Yeh. Your game is up, Ben; I'm locking you up when I get to town. I'll charge you with murder tomorrow."

It was a few minutes after midnight when they carried him back to the cell block.

"I want you to drag out a cot, Oats, and spend the night here," Jim said when the two of them returned to the office. "If Wyeth brings a drunk in you go back with him when he locks him up. Don't let him talk to Ben. I'll wait until you go out and get some supper."

"Anything you say," Oats agreed. "But you ain't goin' to be able to keep the news back that we got Riley locked up. It'll be all over town in a few hours."

"If I can hold it back till morning I'll be satisfied. Bring me a pot of coffee and a couple sandwiches."

"Will that be enough for you?"

"It'll have to be; I don't want to waste time sitting in a restaurant. Late as it is, I'm going to route out Longyear and walk him over to Dan's place. Before I close my eyes I want to know exactly what I'm going to do tomorrow."

Chapter Fourteen

A DARING PLAN

It was after one when Jim banged on Dan Corbett's door. The doctor was used to being called at all hours of the night, but he hardly expected to find the sheriff and district attorney calling on him.

"What's up?" he asked, glancing from one to the other and trying to find his answer before either spoke.

"That's what I'd like to know," Longyear complained irascibly. "Dragging a man out of bed at this time of night!"

"I couldn't see any sense in telling my story twice," said Jim. "Pull down the shades, Dan, and I'll begin."

Ignoring the increasingly hostile interruptions that came from Otis as he proceeded, he gave them a detailed account of what had happened at Mullhall's ranch and Spanish Ford. Before he was finished Otis Longyear was beside himself, his thin face chalk-white with indignation, and when he learned that Little Ben Riley had been placed in jail he could not contain himself any longer.

"Lord, do you actually mean to tell me you've had all this evidence against Ben Riley and failed to consult me?"

"Take it easy," Jim told him. "If I've got any evidence against him it's circumstantial. If you'd issued a warrant on him he'd have slipped through your fingers and the gang would have got rid of him. I know he's guilty, but the only thing we can hold him on is suspicion."

"Have you tried to get a confession?"

"He's ten times as afraid of the vengeance of his own crowd as he is of the law. He won't talk until he knows we've smashed the gang. I've got a lot more to say on some other matters. It's going to gripe you something terrible. But you want to remember that you laughed when Kize tried to tell you we were up against an organized ring of thugs. If he had told the half of what he knew nothing would have done you but to order arrests that would have got us nowhere. I know a public prosecutor hasn't much leeway; the law has spelled out the rules for you. That's why I've kept my mouth shut. I figured when I was sure I could break the case I'd dump the facts in your lap, and you couldn't miss. My hand's been forced. I'm not ready for a showdown, but I've got to risk it. I know it's now or never. That's why I'm talking tonight."

What he had had to say about Little Ben and the information he proceeded to disclose regarding

185

the slaying of such men as Dutch Ritter and Tom Yancey had a stunning effect on Longyear, but it was as nothing compared to the bombshell he exploded when he told him how Kize and Chuck Silvey had been murdered. The D.A. rocked back and forth in his chair too bewildered and infuriated to be able to speak for a minute. Gasping, he popped to his feet and strode back and forth, muttering incoherently.

"You better get hold of yourself, Otis," Dan warned, honestly concerned. "You're a young man, but there's a limit to what your heart will stand."

"I can't believe it!" Longyear wailed. "I can't believe that a man I trusted and depended on to keep me informed could go behind my back and pursue a course that makes an utter idiot of me! I was entitled to know the truth! It was Lord's duty to keep me informed! My God, I'll be the laughingstock of the county!"

"Quit worrying about yourself and try to grasp what all this means," Dan advised sharply. "Nobody's gone behind your back or made a fool of you. Jim's done things the law wouldn't permit you to do. If you convict Morgan and the rest of his gang and send some of them down to Carson City to be hanged and the rest for long prison terms the whole state will be talking about you; you can have anything you want next election."

Jim waited, saying nothing further. Otis began to get hold of himself. He got out a handkerchief and mopped his face.

"Con Morgan!" he got out incredulously. "I never suspected him. How sure are you, Jim?"

"I'm dead sure. He was on pretty safe ground when things started; he'd been here a long time and made a lot of friends. I don't know whether he sent for Silvey and Jenkins and the rest of them. Chances are he didn't have to; the rush was on, and that kind of vermin was sure to show up. He had a ranch. He knew the price of beef would go sky-high. So he fired his old crew and put these thugs on Bar 66. They were road agents, but when they weren't busy at that they filled in their time with a little rustling."

"What about Ben Riley? He was around town for months before there was any talk about gold in Rustlers' Bend. He seemed to be harmless. How did he get mixed up in this?"

"I don't know, Otis," Jim answered frankly. "But I'll make a guess. I believe Little Ben and Morgan were acquainted before either of them showed up in Rock Creek. Little Ben's been a key man. Morgan wouldn't have taken a chance on him if he hadn't known who he was dealing with. He never took a chance on anything. As soon as Little Ben tipped him off that Yancey was on his way to town to identify the parties that killed Jeff Foraker for Kize he ordered Silvey to kill him. Later when he figured that Kize had something on Silvey, he had Silvey killed. And to make it really good he wrote Kize's ticket, too."

Longyear lowered himself into his chair, shaking his head soberly. "You tell a convincing story," he declared. "Can you prove it?"

"Not all of it. Dan's made some interesting experiments. I'll let him explain that part of it."

Corbett produced the slugs he had examined and repeated what he had previously told Oats and Jim. He expected Longyear to take violent exception to the work he had done. To his amazement and Jim's, the district attorney was elated.

"Marvelous!" he exclaimed. "The best kind of evidence I could have!" He checked his enthusiastic outburst suddenly. "It's unfortunate," he continued with a rasp of annoyance, "that the slugs you can identify all come from the guns of men who are dead. But if I can prove there was a connection between Morgan and Silvey and Jenkins the slugs will be very important." He glanced at Jim. "This missing gun that killed Kize and Silvey—have you any idea where to look for it?"

"Just a guess, Otis. Maybe you better call it a hunch. I believe it's Duke Legrand's gun— Morgan's foreman at Bar 66."

The district attorney settled down to putting

together all the facts and surmises Jim had given him. Bringing Wild Bill into court for assault on Riley was such a trifling matter now that he wisely said it better be forgotten for the present. He wanted to know if Morgan and the men on his ranch comprised, in the sheriff's opinion, all of the members of the gang.

"They're the important ones, but I certainly think Con's got two or three or four men right here in town who take their orders from him."

After giving the matter some more thought Longyear said, "I'm trying to size up the whole picture from the legal end. Have I got your word for it that you aren't holding anything back on me?"

"Absolutely! I'm not holding back anything now. It's too late for that. You sound a little dubious about what's been said. Can't you see it?"

"Certainly I can see it!" Otis replied with a sharp note of rebuke. "I'm not thick! I'm sure you've got it sized up correctly. But I'm telling you, Jim, we've still got a lot of work to do. I can hand you a bunch of John Doe warrants in the morning, and you can arrest Morgan and all the rest of them. It won't get us anywhere; we can't charge them with robbery and murder. It'll have to be on suspicion of the same. Pat Holman, Con's lawyer, will have them out of jail in a day or two. They'll be hard to find after that."

"I know all that, and I don't propose to play it that way," Jim declared hotly, at the end of his patience. "There isn't time to do any more work; we've got to take a chance with what we've got. I don't want any John Doe warrants. The biggest mistake we could make right now would be to take Morgan and that bunch up at the ranch into custody. What we want to do is put the panic on them—watch the railroad and the roads and stop anyone who tries to run. Morgan will know in a few hours—he may know this minute—that we've got Ben Riley locked up and why. It'll scare Morgan, but he won't lose his wits; he'll have Holman busy in the morning trying to spring Little Ben on a writ. If you can fight him off for twenty-four hours I'll pull the rug out from under all of them."

"I can head off a habeas corpus for a day or two," Longyear said flatly, "but I'm not at all convinced that you can put evidence enough together in that time to convict them. You've got something in mind. What is it?"

"I'm going to ask Iris to devote most of the front page of the *Enterprise* tomorrow to a straight news story that'll say everything I've said tonight —name names, accuse Morgan of being the headman of this bandit ring, and make it so strong it'll blow the lid off of everything. She can quote me, and I hope you'll have the guts to let her quote you."

The district attorney threw up his hands in horror.

"That's the most fantastic, rattlebrained thing I ever heard! You can't print surmises and suspicions as fact! That's libel!"

"Libel, your grandmother!" Jim rapped. His restraint had snapped, and he was a fearsome figure as he glowered at Otis. "Morgan owns the *Enterprise*. He can't be libeled by his own newspaper. Iris can word what you say so you'll be covered. As for myself, I don't care; if a blast like that doesn't shake Morgan loose I'll hand in my resignation."

"I'm afraid you will be handing in your resignation, too, Otis," Corbett volunteered. "Strikes me you're caught between the devil and deep blue sea. The camp's fading. The gold excitement will be over in a week or two. These crooks will leave for parts unknown, and you'll be left holding the bag—all these crimes unsolved and no one brought to justice. If that happens you couldn't be elected dog catcher. Jim's idea is wild and risky, but it may turn the trick. I believe it will. If the *Enterprise* comes out with a story like that it'll stand this town on its head. I know Morgan's a shrewd customer, but if he doesn't make a false move and give himself away when a story like that breaks, nothing will do it."

Longyear continued to shake his head. "It's impossible! Iris would never consent to it."

"I sounded her out on it," Jim told him. "I think she *can* be persuaded."

"She couldn't get away with it if she wanted to," Otis persisted. "Morgan would get wind of it and stop her."

"You leave that to Dan and me; we'll see that she has all the protection she needs and that no tales are carried down the street to Morgan till the paper's off the press." Jim jerked to his feet, his lean fighting face tense and uncompromising. "I'm not going to sit here all night arguing with you, Otis. All you're fighting for is your job and political career. I'm fighting for my job, too, but that's the small end of it with me; I want to square Kize's account in full. I've got a dozen reliable men lined up that I can swear in at a minute's notice. I'll have them block every road, and I'll post a couple at the depot. I'll stay close to Morgan myself. In the meantime Oats will take a bunch of men and go up through Squaw Hills and plant them where they can keep the Bar 66 house under surveillance. All you've got to do is decide which way you want to jump and do it now."

"I'm not going to be bulldozed into anything," Otis said flatly. "I'll sleep on this and give you my answer in the morning."

"No, you won't," Jim contradicted. "I've got to know now. When I leave here I'm going to see Iris. I want this to be all set before I turn in.

192

Morgan's spies will be watching us by morning. I'm not going near the *Enterprise* tomorrow till the paper's out, and I want you to keep away. Good heavens, Otis, you've got everything to win and nothing to lose. If it's credit you want, you'll get it; you're on record with the commissioners as having information so important that you refused to divulge it even to them. That's proof enough that you were in this from the first. Kize and me made the snowballs, but it's up to you to throw them."

This appeal to the district attorney's vanity was a telling argument. After some hesitation he said he'd go through with it.

"But you have Iris come to the courthouse in the morning and let me read her supposed interview with me," he insisted. "She's in my office every morning. There won't be anything suspicious about that."

"All right," Jim agreed. "I'll ask her to have it all on paper when she sees you."

The conference broke up presently, and Jim went on to the Farraday home. A discreet tapping on a bedroom window awakened Iris.

"It's me—Jim," he told her. "I've got to see you. Just slip something on and don't bother to put on your war paint."

He acquainted her with all that had happened in the past few hours and what had passed between Longyear and himself.

"And Otis has agreed to it?" she asked, not hiding her surprise.

"He wants you to write out what you're going to say over his name. You can put any words in my mouth that you please; I don't care how far you go. You can have your story finished by noon. If you hand it to the compositors when they come back from dinner, how long will it take them to set it?"

"About two hours."

"That'll give you all the time you need. Dan has agreed to show up at your office at one o'clock and stay with you until the paper's out. He'll lock the back door and see that no one leaves the building."

He mentioned the other precautions he was taking: deputizing a number of men, sending Oats to Bar 66, and guarding the roads and railroad depot.

"I'll keep Morgan in sight all afternoon," he ran on. "You don't have to be afraid of him, Iris; if he makes a beeline for the *Enterprise* as soon as he reads the paper I won't be far away. What do you say? Will you do your part?"

"Yes," she answered simply, "and I'll be thinking of Dad with every line I write."

Chapter Fifteen

OUTLAW GANG EXPOSED

Oats had his cot put away and the office swept before seven and was getting anxious about his breakfast when Jim walked in. "Well," he drawled, looking the sheriff over carefully, "if I can read the signs, you're all spooked up this mornin'. What's doin'?"

"I'm sitting on a keg of gunpowder with a short fuse, that's all," Jim answered. He knew Oats had to be told exactly how things stood, and in detail, for a great deal was to depend on the redhead.

Some of it came as no surprise to Oats, but to learn that Jim's plans were completed and the next few hours were to bring the showdown left him a bit goggled-eyed.

"Where do I fit into it?" he asked.

"I'm going to deputize half a dozen men for you and send you to Bar 66. Watch the house. See who comes. Maybe no one will. I'm going to post a couple men on the short cut up through the hills. Don't let anyone leave. Stop 'em with gunfire if nothing else will do. And stay up there till I join you. Take my binoculars. You can lay back far enough so you won't be spotted. You got all that?"

"Sure! When do I pull away?"

"In an hour or two. You bothered last night?"

"No, I didn't see anybody. Riley's askin' for a lawyer. Says he wants Pat Holman."

"He does, eh?" Jim smiled mirthlessly. "That saves Morgan the embarrassment of going out on the limb for him. I'll get word to Holman later in the morning. I've had breakfast; you go out and get yours. And no gabbing, Oats."

By eight-thirty he had his deputies sworn in. They were instructed to take up their various positions quietly shortly after noon. He mentioned the men who were to be turned back if they attempted to leave town. After he had selected the deputies who were to go with Oats he had a word or two with the redhead.

"Drift out of town, a couple at a time," he advised. "You can rendezvous up the trail at the old cabin. That'll hold down the talk."

"You got any idea when I'll be seein' you?" Oats asked.

"It'll depend on how things go at this end."

Oats nodded. "I'll tell the boys about gettin' away." His eyes found Jim's for a moment. "Take care of yourself," he said. It was as near as he had ever come to expressing his warm feeling for Jim Lord.

After they were gone Jim went down the street

and looked in at the Maverick saloon and the hotel. Morgan was conspicuous by his absence. Nor was anything to be seen of Slip Egan and several others who were suspect. Otherwise—to a casual observer—the life of the town might have seemed to pursue its usual pattern this morning. Jim looked deeper than that, and below the surface he caught a vague tension and sober expectancy, as though Rock Creek was girding itself for some violent upheaval.

Everyone knew by now that Little Ben Riley had been taken into custody. While no specific charge had been filed against him as yet, tales reaching town from the Bend left no doubt as to why he had been arrested.

"That's the reason," Jim said to himself, seeking an explanation for the lurking uneasiness he read in men's faces. "They know that throwing Riley into the pokey will bring other develop-ments."

He was positive that his own plans had not leaked. Leaving the hotel, he crossed the street and climbed the stairs to Pat Holman's office and told him Little Ben wanted to see him. The lawyer pretended to be surprised, but Jim was sure in his own mind that Morgan had already communicated with the man.

"If you're going back to the jail I'll walk around with you," said Holman.

At the corner Jim saw Iris going up the courthouse steps. He glanced at his watch and was pleased to discover that she was on time to the minute for her daily round of the county offices. The importance of her errand this morning had not thrown her off stride. In his eyes it spoke volumes for her courage and self-control.

Holman conferred with Little Ben for twenty minutes or more. When the lawyer walked into Jim's office his attitude was belligerent. "What's the charge going to be?" he demanded.

"Suspicion of murder."

Holman snorted contemptuously. "You can't hold him without giving him a hearing. I'll see Messenger right away and demand that Riley be brought before him tomorrow morning."

"Go to it," Jim told him. "I can hold Ben on suspicion for two or three days. By then I may be able to present some evidence that'll prevent you from springing him."

Cap Wyeth, the town marshal, sauntered in soon after the lawyer left. He was full of questions. "Little Ben was always ready to do a man a favor," he said. "I sorta cottoned to him. I can't believe he was mixed up in all these killin's and robberies. Yuh actually think yuh got a case ag'in him?"

"Well, I've got him locked up," Jim replied. "That should speak for itself."

"Yeh," Cap muttered. "Do yuh mind if I go back and talk to him?"

"I mind a lot. Pat Holman's been talking to him. I can't keep his lawyer out, but no one else is going to see him."

"Hunh!" Cap snorted, affronted. "That's purty high-handed, ain't it?"

"You can think what you please about it," said Jim. "That's the way I'm playing it."

After Cap left Jim took his chair outside and sat down beside the door as Kize had been wont to do. He had been there only a short while when he saw Joe Sherdell coming up the walk. Like himself, Joe was an ex-cowpuncher. He had set up in business as Rock Creek's iceman. Of the eleven men Jim had sworn in that morning, Joe was the only one with previous experience as a part-time deputy.

"I've got everythin' set," Joe announced. "Fred Coles is goin' to take over my route for me. I can stick it out here as long as necessary now." He took off his hat and wiped his forehead. "A mite hot for this time of year." He laughed and added, "That's always good for my business."

"It's a beautiful day, for sure," Jim observed. "I asked you to stay here, Joe, because I know I can count on you. I'll be in and out of the office most of the day. No one but Pat Holman is to talk with Riley—that's unless he asks for the doctor. It'll be all right to let Corbett see him. Understand?"

Sherdell nodded.

"I'll spell you for half an hour at mealtime," Jim continued. "If I'm down the street and someone comes with word that I want you don't fall for it; it'll be a trick to get to Riley."

"You think they may try to bust him out?"

"I don't know what they'd do if they get to him. Maybe they'd kill him in his cell to shut his mouth. Just watch yourself, Joe. If the break comes it'll be late in the afternoon."

"If?" Joe echoed. He gave Jim a thin smile. "You don't sound to me as though there was any 'if' in it."

Jim shrugged. "We'll see."

The morning wore on. Just before noon Dave McGheean, the Rock Creek postmaster, came to get Little Ben's keys. He was going up to the Bend, he said, with a new man to take Riley's place. "I hope I find his accounts with the department in order."

"I think you will," Jim told him. "Ben had bigger fish to fry than filching from the government. I'll get the keys."

There was a short-order restaurant around the corner that had a contract with the county to serve meals to the prisoners. A boy arrived with a tray for Riley just before twelve. Sherdell took it back to the cell, and Jim left to get his own dinner. He was gone no more than half an hour. It was the deputy's turn then. Joe was back a few minutes after one.

"I just saw Corbett goin' into the *Enterprise*," he told Jim.

"Good!" the sheriff said. "Everything seems to be going according to schedule."

As he surmised, Dan found Iris waiting for him.

"Do you want to read this stuff before I give it to the compositors?" she asked.

"No," Dan told her, remarking to himself how cool she was. "I know you went all out."

"I did," Iris admitted. "It's my swan song, and I made it a good one. The *Enterprise* will be a ship without a rudder by evening."

"And very likely without a captain," Dan supplemented.

The mechanical staff of the newspaper was limited to four men—two compositors, Lem Galloway, the pressman, and Clint Eddy, his assistant.

Dan and Iris walked into the pressroom, which was separated from the offices by a wooden partition. While she was conferring with her compositors he locked the back door and pocketed the key. The six windows were barred with heavy wire gratings. Anyone attempting to leave the room would have to pass through the door to the offices.

The two men who were to set the story were immediately excited by the "copy" Iris handed them. They looked up at her aghast.

"You—you out of your mind, Miz Farraday?" one of them gasped.

"No, Sam, I know what I'm doing," she answered calmly. "You and Charlie get to work. Doctor Corbett is going to sit here until the paper is being distributed to the boys."

As soon as the office door closed on her Galloway and his assistant dropped what they were doing and crowded around the compositors, who regaled them with snatches of the story.

"Goddlemighty!" Lem Galloway groaned. "Con Morgan! Who'd have thought it?"

His assistant, Clint Eddy, was no less excited.

"Well, boys, you've got a paper to get out," Dan said from his chair near the door. "You better get busy."

It was warm in the pressroom. When he removed his coat they saw that he wore a gun. It was an unusual circumstance, and the air in the room began to grow electric.

Galloway and Eddy inked the rollers of the flatbed press and locked up the forms on the pages that were already in type. Several times young Eddy's eyes strayed to the padlocked back door. Dan caught it. He knew that Eddy was making sure it was locked. It confirmed the suspicion in Dan's mind that the assistant pressman was the man to watch. He was not surprised forty minutes later when, with the press standing waiting, Eddy grabbed his cap and started to hurry past him.

"Sorry, Clint," Dan told him, "but no one's leaving till the paper's on the street."

"I was just going out to get a pack of cigarettes," Eddy protested. "I won't be gone five minutes."

"No," Corbett said flatly. "You're not tipping Morgan off. You better begin asking yourself which side of the bread your butter is on. Con Morgan's friends are going to be very unpopular in Rock Creek in another hour or two."

Eddy grew belligerent and stoutly denied there was any connection between Con and himself. Dan listened until he had heard all he cared to hear. "That's enough," he said with finality. "Hang up your cap, Clint; you're in for the afternoon."

That ended it. Still sulking, Eddy walked back to the metal-topped table where Lem Galloway, who could do most anything around a newspaper plant, was setting the eight-column head Iris had laid out.

As soon as the story itself was in type it was proofed at once and passed through the wicket to Iris. When she had proofread it she brought it in and complimented the men on the speed they had made. Lem had the head ready. She had a look at it.

"All right," she said. "Lock up, Lem, and let her roll. We'll give them something to talk about over the supper table tonight."

Jim was seated in the lobby of the hotel when he saw the boys dart away from the *Enterprise* with the day's edition. They were as wild and excited as young eagles. Their excitement was mild compared to their customers' when the latter glimpsed the headlines that screamed:

Outlaw Gang Exposed

Wholesale Arrests Promised.
District Attorney and Sheriff Reveal Truth About Killing of Kize Farraday and Others

Con Morgan Alleged Mastermind of Bandit Ring

One of the youngsters dashed into the hotel and slapped a bundle of papers on the desk. The clerk started to glance at them with a bored air. He was suddenly electrified by what his eyes saw. After staring transfixed at the headlines for a moment he threw off his trance and bolted through the door to Morgan's private office. There was silence within for a few seconds, then Morgan's voice raised in an enraged bellow so violent that the very air seemed to rock. Bursting from his office, coatless and unarmed, the crumpled copy of the *Enterprise* clutched in his fist, and stopping not even to grab his hat, he stormed out of the hotel, bound for the news-paper office.

The little building that housed the *Enterprise* stood on the corner a short block away. If Con's first thought had been to reach it in time to stop the distribution of the edition he must have known before he got halfway there that he was too late. Men got in his path and refused to step aside, their hostility engraved in every feature of their dark faces and ready to crystallize into action as soon as they recovered from their surprise.

Jim followed closely, and he was at the corner when Morgan reached the door of the *Enterprise.* He could see Iris seated at her desk. Nothing was to be seen of Dan, but he was certain the doctor was only a few steps away behind the partition.

Knowing Corbett would protect Iris, Jim stopped at the corner, trying to gauge the temper of the town. Rock Creek was going wild. The same mob fury that had gripped the men at Spanish Ford could be very easily fanned into a raging fire here.

Iris saw Morgan coming. She spoke to Dan, and he told her not to be afraid. A moment later Morgan rushed in, his cavernous rocky face pasty-white with rage.

"You'll pay for this!" he roared. "You'll pay for your damned lies, and so'll Longyear and Jim Lord!" He slapped her face with his folded copy of the *Enterprise.* Catching her by the shoulder, his fingers ripping her waist, he pulled her to her feet. "Now get out of here, you double-crossing little bitch!"

He gave her a shove that sent her reeling toward the door. Dan stepped in too late to catch her, but Bill Mullhall's bulk filled the doorway, and he caught her. There was a cold fury in the man that was more forbidding by far than Con Morgan's booming wrath.

"He shouldn't have done that, Miss Farraday," said Bill, his voice harsh and merciless. "He shouldn't have talked to you that way neither; you're a lady, if he ever saw one. But don't let it bother you too much; it'll be one of the last things he'll ever say."

He handed her over to Dan and started for Morgan. The latter backed away until he had the wall behind him and could retreat no farther. There was terror in Con's eyes.

"I ain't armed!" he whined.

Bill didn't bother to answer. He brought his right hand up from the knees and sent an iron fist crashing into Morgan's jaw, lifting him to his toes and driving his head against the wall with a crunching thud that rocked Morgan's senses. Wrapping his fingers in the collar of Con's shirt, Bill dragged him to the street.

As Jim stood on the corner Wild Bill, Cass Curry, and two other Mullhall men had brushed past him, walking rapidly, their faces hard and tense. To his surprise they had stopped at the door of the newspaper office and Bill had hurried in. It was only then that Jim understood why Curry carried a coiled lariat.

When Mullhall dragged Morgan out he found the sheriff facing him. Bill had no intention of being stopped. "Toss your rope over the limb of this cottonwood, Curry!" he growled. "We'll finish off this pup here and now!"

"Bill, Morgan belongs to me." Jim spoke with a quiet authority, his face hard and flat. "You haven't got backing enough to get away with this. The law's bigger than you, just as Kize told you."

"Yeh, he told me—and what did it get him? If he'd listened to me he'd be alive today! You goin' to make the same damned fool mistake, too?"

As they stood there toe to toe, neither ready to give an inch, Curry dropped his rope over the limb of the cottonwood.

"Well," Mullhall rapped, "how do you want it?"

"Don't force my hand," Jim returned. "You owe me a favor, Bill. Last night—remember?"

That put another face on it with Mullhall. "I remember," he said through clenched teeth, a frosty glitter in his eyes. "I was savin' it for a time when I figgered you'd really need it." He gave Morgan a shove in Jim's direction. "Take him, if you got to be a sucker!"

Con had not opened his mouth. His cheeks were sagging as though he had shot in them. When Jim grabbed him by the arm and led him away he didn't protest. It was a different story when they turned the courthouse corner and the crowd that had been following them held back.

"I'll make you and Longyear eat the bluff you're throwing!" he ground out savagely. "Lies and hot air—that's all it is! You can't lock me up!"

"Can't I?" Jim challenged, his voice razor-edged. "I just saved your rotten neck. I'll lock you up and keep you locked up."

On reaching the office he told Joe to search Morgan for a knife or other weapons. They found nothing. After removing the prisoner's suspenders and necktie they marched him back to the cell block and locked him up, to the speechless amazement of Little Ben.

"I want to see Holman," Con growled. "Get him here right away!"

"You'll see Holman tomorrow morning—not before," Jim informed him.

Chapter Sixteen

CLEAN GETAWAY

Sheriff Lord read the *Enterprise* story hurriedly but without skipping a line. From across the desk Joe Sherdell said, "We got two of 'em in the cooler now. Looks like we was doin' all right."

"It's too early to say," Jim returned soberly. "I didn't plan on having to lock up Morgan. Mullhall forced that on me; he and some of his crowd had the gall to think they could give Con a ride at the end a of rope right on the main street of Rock Creek. A man can hardly do anything to give himself away when he's behind bars." Jim shook his head regretfully. "I was counting on Con to do something that would be a giveaway."

From a closet in the corner of the office he produced old Kize's sawed-off shotgun and a bag of shells.

"Keep this handy," he told Joe. "Wild Bill listened to my argument a few minutes ago, but he may get to talking it up again. It'll sound good to some, no doubt. I'm going to stop in at the *Enterprise* for a minute and then go on to the depot. I've got a little time before the evening train pulls out."

He found Iris cleaning out her desk preparatory to leaving the *Enterprise* office for what might be the last time, or certainly for as long as Con Morgan owned the paper. Corbett was with her, tying the books and papers she wanted to take home into a bundle.

"Jim!" she cried, rushing into his arms.

He held her close for a moment. He could see that the strain she had been under was telling on her; her face looked drawn, and her lips had lost their long alluring curve.

"You did a swell job, honey," he said, his voice as tender as it was sober. "I didn't figure Mullhall would bust in on you."

Dan spoke up. "It's a good thing he did. I was asleep at the switch, letting Morgan slap her around like that."

"He paid for it," Iris declared firmly. "Of all the men in the world Wild Bill Mullhall was the last one I would have expected to come to my rescue and defend me like that." She shook her head at the memory. "I've always had an aversion to fighting, but when I saw him drive his fist into Con Morgan's jaw I could have screamed with delight." She looked up and tried to read Jim's eyes. "Having to arrest Morgan isn't going to help your chances, is it?"

"No," he admitted. "My best hope now is that he got someone through to the ranch. If Legrand and the rest of them start to run, that could do the trick. I'm going down to the depot and see if anybody tries to slip out on the evening train. You're about ready to leave?"

"In a few minutes, Jim. Dan is going to walk me home. You'll have to hurry if you want to be at the depot in time."

"Wait a second," Dan interjected as Jim started out. "What about some protection for Iris? I've got patients to look after. I'll be free this evening, but that isn't enough."

"You're right," Jim agreed. "After the train pulls out I'll send the two boys I've got posted there up to the house, Iris. They can spell each other and spend the night on the porch."

"Jim, that isn't necessary. I'm sure I'll be all right."

"We'll play it safe," he told her. "You know Carl Henry and Tony Kelland. They'll take good care of you."

At the depot he spoke to the two deputies. They had seen nothing of the men suspected of being Morgan adherents. The train was due to pull out in a few minutes. Most of the passengers were already aboard. Jim swung up at the rear and walked through the coaches and the smoker. Slip Egan and the two or three others who might have taken this means of getting away from Rock Creek were not in the cars. The possibility of their making a last moment's rush for the train did not escape Jim. He told his deputies to be on the watch for it.

The train pulled out, however, without their showing up.

"Maybe we're having better luck elsewhere," he said to Henry and Kelland. Doubt was beginning to assail him. He put it out of his mind and told the two men to get their supper. Afterward they were to look out for Iris until he relieved them in the morning.

There were only three roads and the trail through the Squaw Hills leading out of Rock Creek. Borrowing a horse, he made the rounds of them, questioning the men he had on guard. He met the same answer everywhere. Egan and the other suspects had made no attempt to pass the roadblocks.

Concealing his disappointment, he ordered his deputies to maintain their vigil throughout the night. Turning back to town, he stopped at the courthouse and went up to see the district attorney. He found him pacing the floor, his nerves worn ragged.

"I've been waiting for some word from you," Otis snapped. "I heard about Mullhall and Morgan. What about the others?"

"Nothing doing so far." Jim eased himself into a chair. "They're sitting tight. We'll have to wait them out."

"Wait them out! Wait them out!" Longyear exploded. "You were so positive there'd be a break as soon as they read the paper. All we've done is expose our hand for nothing. We can't hold Morgan more than a day or two. Why did you have to arrest him?"

"To save his neck. He wouldn't be much good to us dangling from the limb of that cottonwood. If you're thinking of telling me to turn him loose, forget it. He'd be strung up inside of an hour. If you've been down the street you know what the feeling is. Rock Creek believes every word it reads in the *Enterprise*."

Longyear flopped into his swivel chair and swung back and forth, his face working nervously. "What are we going to do?" he demanded contentiously. "We can't just wait."

"That's all you can do," Jim said thinly as he reached for his hat. "I'm going to Bar 66 as soon as I grab a bite to eat. We don't know what the situation is there. It may be all in our favor. The best thing you can do, Otis, is to keep your rompers on till we know for certain where we stand."

While Jim was seated at the counter in Tate's short-order restaurant Oliver Failes, Woodhull's Double Diamond foreman, walked in and took the stool beside him. Failes was a man of parts and just the person the sheriff felt he needed to stand guard at the jail with Sherdell. After they had exchanged a word or two he said, "Are you going to be in town overnight, Ollie?"

"Yeh. The boss's wife is comin' up from Reno

213

on the mornin' train. I'm goin' to drive her out to the ranch. Why do you ask?"

Jim explained what he wanted. "I may be seeing trouble where there isn't any. On the other hand Mullhall is still in town. If he gets to blowing off he might steam up a crowd. I'll be away for a few hours; I'm going up to Bar 66. I wouldn't be calling on you otherwise, Ollie."

"That's all right," Failes told him. "I've got to order some provisions for the ranch so they'll be ready for me to pick up in the morning. You tell Joe I'll be down in thirty, forty minutes."

After explaining to Sherdell that the Double Diamond foreman would join him for the night Jim went back to the barn and saddled a horse. He was well up the Squaw Hills trail when night fell. Being careful to make noise enough to telegraph his coming ahead of him, he proceeded until he was within less than half a mile of the Bar 66 house before he was suddenly commanded to pull up and hoist his hands.

"Who are you?" a voice demanded gruffly from the cover of a patch of mahogany bush.

Jim thought he recognized the voice. "Sheriff Lord," he answered.

"Oh, hell!" came a cry of dismay from the shadows. "Just you! I figgered I'd snagged somebody!"

The man stepped out into the open. He was

Slim Haller, one of the deputies who had come up from town with Oats.

"What's doing up here?" Jim asked.

"Nuthin', so far as I know," Slim answered. "Oats is off to the left a couple hundred yards. I was just makin' a little scout over this way when I heard you comin'."

Together they moved on to where Oats and the other deputies were gathered. The redhead could only repeat what Slim had said.

"Been quiet as a graveyard," he complained. "We been here for hours circlin' the house and keepin' to the brush. Legrand and the rest of 'em have been fiddlin' around the yard and the corrals all day. No one's come up from town. If Morgan sent a man up, he got here ahead of us."

"That isn't likely," said Jim, his keen disappointment evident. "I've got Morgan locked up. If I had had any idea that was going to be necessary I'd have left the trail wide open. But if they're still *here,* that's something; if they'd been tipped off some of them would have tried to make a run for it by now."

He brought Oats up to date on what had occurred in town. As he talked he watched the house. Buttery daubs of light shone from the windows.

"Slim had the idea this afternoon," said Oats, "that mebbe these birds had a set of signals rigged up and that it wasn't necessary for anyone to reach the house to tip 'em off that the jig was up."

"What did you mean, Slim?" Jim inquired. "A series of shots?"

"No, smoke or some sort of wigwaggin'. We saw Legrand out in the yard usin' a pair of glasses. I figgered he wasn't tryin' to find out what time of day it was."

"Could be," Jim was forced to admit. "I suppose a man on top of Coulter's Knob could be seen from the house with a good pair of binoculars. But if they knew the bottom had dropped out of their game they would have pulled away as soon as it got dark; Legrand's too smart to think for a minute that he could save himself by forting up in the house. We'll stick it out and see what happens."

The night wore on. It got to be ten o'clock. The lights in the Bar 66 house continued to burn. Ranch house lights didn't usually burn that late. The circumstance struck Jim as suspicious. Half an hour later inaction and the growing feeling that Longyear had been right when he said they had exposed their hand for nothing forced him to a decision.

"We're going in," he announced. "We'll leave our broncs here and creep up on foot. There's eight of us. We'll spread out and converge on the kitchen door. When the first shot comes drop down and hug the ground."

The men voiced their approval; they were tired of waiting, too.

"After that first blast we move up a bit, and when we're close to the door we make a rush for it—is that it?" Oats asked.

"No, we won't rush 'em," Jim replied. "We'll stay put and just throw enough lead at the house to hold them here till morning. I'll bring enough men up to surround the place and make capture certain."

They advanced carefully until they were in easy range. The night continued as silent and peaceful as ever. Continuing to close in, they reached the corrals and found themselves within seventy-five yards of the kitchen, and still not a gun had flashed from window or door.

It seemed queer to Jim. He called softly to Oats and moved him over for a word.

"The corrals—no more horses in 'em than that this afternoon?"

"There was three times as many!" Oats growled apprehensively after a long glance.

"I thought so!" Jim muttered.

"What do you mean?" The question was superfluous; Oats knew what he meant.

"No one here!" was the savage response. "Come on!"

Jim threw caution away and marched up boldly to the door and kicked it open. Oats followed him in, and the others were only a step behind. Their entrance went unopposed. In a few minutes they had searched the house. They had it to themselves.

"Pulled out! Made a clean getaway!" Slim Haller's voice was shrill with anger and disgust.

Jim felt the stove. It was cold. "They've been gone some time," he said.

Oats was inconsolable, blaming himself for the gang's escape.

"Stop it!" Jim snapped, more annoyed with himself than with Oats. "It wasn't your fault. Slim was right, I reckon; they used signals. I noticed the last time I was here there's a shallow ravine leads up the ridge. That's the way they must have gone, leading their broncs till they were over the crest. All they had to do then was drop down through the Blue Meadows and head for Idaho."

"We can go after them," Oats growled. "No use standin' here gabbin'!"

Jim shook his head. "No use chasing them. Too late for that; they're well on their way to the line by now. The best thing I can do is to get back to town and telegraph every Idaho sheriff along the southern tier to be on the lookout for them."

He had scarcely finished speaking when Slim doused the light. "Someone comin'!" he jerked out sharply. "Broncs runnin'!"

They listened and discovered he was correct.

"Keep away from the windows till we find out what this is!" Jim ordered.

They caught the sharp reining in of horses, and then a voice yelled, "Hello the house!"

Jim ran to the door. "Dan, is that you?"

"Yes! Thank God we found you!" Corbett called back. "Light a lamp!"

It was only a moment before he tramped into the kitchen. With him came Wild Bill, Cass Curry, and half a dozen others. What Mullhall was doing riding with Dan, Jim and Oats didn't know. They were to find out a moment later.

"We just got into the house and found it empty," Jim told the newcomers. "Legrand and every last one of them gave us the slip."

"We knew before you did!" Wild Bill rapped. "They rode into town a little better'n an hour ago and took Morgan and Riley out of the jail. They're on the way to Mount Misery, the whole eleven of 'em. If we're goin' after 'em, let's get started!"

"Wait a minute," Jim got out, his voice husky with chagrin and failure. "Tell me exactly what happened, Dan."

"They were clever about it," Corbett said. "Cap Wyeth brought Slip Egan in for being drunk and disorderly. There's no reason to think Cap was in on the game, but Egan wasn't drunk. He broke away from Cap in your office. Sherdell and Ollie started to give the marshal a hand. That was the signal for Legrand and the rest of them to pile in. They had your deputies and Cap covered before they could lift a finger. They got the keys and freed Riley and Morgan. Not a shot was fired. Before they left the jail they pushed Cap and your men into a cell and locked them up. They had left their horses down behind your barn. They had extra ones for Riley and Con. But they didn't pull away at once. Believe it or not, three of them had the crust to walk Con to the hotel. He opened his safe. Got his money, I suppose. It wasn't till then, I understand, that anyone knew they were in town. Before anything could be done Steve Gore and the rest of the gang dashed up with the led horses. It was only a minute or so before the lot of them were riding out of town."

It was a crushing blow. Jim could not completely dissemble its stunning effect, but he refused to accept defeat. "They may have outsmarted themselves. Taking the Mount Misery Road is a feint to draw pursuit in that direction. Beyond the Ashbourn mine that road ends in a tangle of canyons that a horse can't negotiate. If Morgan and Legrand don't know it, Steve Gore does. They may go as far as the mine. If they do, they'll begin cutting back east then."

"East to the Owyhee, you mean, and try to fade away out on the desert?" Dan queried.

"They might, but I don't believe that'll be their play. Rustlers' Bend used to be the short cut to Idaho. It's still there. Gore is familiar enough with it. As long as I've got to gamble, I'll gamble on the Bend. It's just possible we can reach the portal ahead of them. Oats, you and the boys fetch up our broncs! We'll get away as quickly as we can!"

Corbett gave Jim an encouraging slap on the shoulder. "You don't have to take it so hard. You've got them on the run. That cries, 'Guilty!' And what they did in town tonight is further proof of it."

"That's one way to look at it," Jim acknowledged. He glanced at Mullhall. "I'm glad you're riding with us, Bill. You never would talk, either to Kize or me, but you've read the paper. How right was the story?"

"A hundred percent right! I didn't have to come to this country to get acquainted with Duke Legrand and some of the others. When I showed up Morgan offered me a deal if I'd throw in with him. As for sayin' anythin' to Kize or you—how could I? It was never my pattern to go blabbin' to the law or playin' stool pigeon. As for turnin' road agent, hell! I fought 'em for too many years to want any part of that. You'll save a few minutes if you go up through my place and cut across the Idaho Road to the portal. I don't see a rifle in the crowd. We can get 'em at the ranch. Six-guns won't be heavy enough for this job."

"Thanks, Bill. We'll need rifles, sure enough." Jim heard the horses coming up. "Come on," he said, "we can get started!"

Chapter Seventeen

AMBUSH IN A GORGE

At Mullhall's ranch the posse got rifles and additional men. Cutting across the meandering Idaho Road, they struck northeast and reached Rock Creek and the upper diggings. Tent flaps were raised as they passed, the gold seekers rushing out to determine the reason for the commotion.

The walls of the rocky gorge down which Rock Creek broke through to the Bend rose sheer for several hundred feet. Beyond was the high plateau that flowed away across the state line to the wide expanse of the uninhabited Snake River Plains. The trail the rustlers had used in the long ago wound up the eastern buttress of the portal; the western approach was, for any practical purpose, unscalable.

Where the ascent began there was a patch of sand. Jim got down and examined it carefully for fresh hoofprints of horses. The moon was in its first quarter and low in the sky, but the stars shone brilliantly, providing light enough for him to be sure of what he found.

"No fresh tracks," he announced. "If this is the way they're coming, we're in time."

They held a brief parley.

"If some of us go to the top and the rest hide out down here we can get that bunch in between us and have 'em dead to rights," said Mullhall.

"That sounds all right to me," Jim declared. "Bill, you and your boys go up the trail. Oats and Slim will go with you. That'll leave me men enough at this end. We'll move back into the brush. There's good cover for you up there, Oats. Get set as soon as you can. We won't show our hand till they pass us. You'll hear a flurry of shots from us then. That'll be the signal for you to open up. If they want to surrender, okay; otherwise start blasting them. Just be sure they don't get through you."

"Hell!" Wild Bill growled. "It'll be as easy as stringin' fish!"

It was already well past midnight. It got to be one o'clock.

"What do you think?" Corbett asked Jim.

"If they're coming, they should be here in the next hour." The anxiety in Dan's voice had not escaped Lord. "This was a gamble from the first. We'll have to keep that in mind."

Two o'clock came, and the brooding stillness of the night was broken only by the yipping of a distant coyote. The moon had long since set. Some of the stars seemed to be winking out.

Jim stuck it out for another quarter of an hour in sullen silence. Finally he said, "Looks like I guessed wrong. We'll hang on for another thirty minutes. If they don't show by then, we'll send word up to Oats and the bunch of us can head back to town."

Less than a quarter of an hour passed when they were electrified to see a cavalcade of horsemen coming up the Bend. They were strung out in twos and riding slowly, obviously saving their horses against the long ride ahead.

"Quiet, now!" Jim warned. "Not a peep out of anybody!"

Steve Gore rode in the lead with Morgan. Jim and the possemen could see him pointing out the old trail up the wall.

All unsuspicious of the danger lurking so close at hand, Morgan and his men started the ascent. They were halfway up before Jim gave word to move out into the trail below them. That movement, careful as it was, dislodged fragments of rock.

It was all the warning the gang needed to tell them something was amiss. A flurry of shots from below, all deliberately wide of the mark, confirmed it. When an answering blast came from above, Morgan's gang realized in a hurry that they had ridden into a trap. Now it was Legrand, not Con, who took charge. "Give these broncs hell and follow me!" he yelled. "We'll smash through that gunfire up there or know why!"

They tried it, but found it so hot they had to turn back. A wounded horse threw its rider. Maddened with pain, the screaming animal darted across the face of the wall, lost its footing in a loose rock fall, and went plunging to its death in the creek far below.

Legrand's next move was to try to break back down the trail. Jim and his men quickly changed the bandit's mind about that. Realizing that they were opposed in force both from above and below, Legrand and his companions flung themselves out of the saddle and sought what shelter they could find among the rock outcroppings. Steve Gore rolled into a pocket that was deep and wide enough for all. In a matter of seconds they crawled in with him and began sniping uphill and down.

Oats and his party began to return the fire with a vengeance. Jim and his possemen did the same. The latter now found themselves in double jeopardy, with the gunfire from the rim as serious a menace as the slugs that whined their way from the pocket where the bandits were holed up. Simply by watching the gun flashes they could tell what was occurring above. Twice within the space of a few minutes Oats and his crowd tried to rush the pocket, only to be thrown back.

"Good God!" Jim cried. "They'll be cut to

ribbons if they don't stop that—to say nothing of mowing us down!" He turned to Charlie Johnson, one of his cowboy deputies. "Charlie, can you get up there? By a roundabout way, I mean."

"Yeh, if I drop down the crick a bit. It'll take some time, but I can make it."

"Get going then and don't let it take you any longer than necessary. Tell Oats I said to hold off till dawn so we can see what we're doing. And you can tell them up there that their slugs are whining all around us. You needn't come back; I have men enough."

Johnson had been gone some time when Oats's and Wild Bill's men made another futile attempt to close in. As the minutes ticked away and the move was not repeated, Jim took it for granted that Johnson had reached them.

The firing continued spasmodically. An hour and more passed. One of Jim's men stopped a bullet. Corbett cut off the man's sleeve to make a tourniquet. He was stopping the flow of blood when Jim bent down beside him.

"Just a bad flesh wound," Dan told him. "We've been lucky so far. How late is it?"

"It's getting on toward four o'clock. It's a long night."

Even after the stars faded dawn seemed a long time in coming. Finally streaks of pink and orange began to play along the eastern horizon.

Down along the creek a ground mist floated in soft swirling layers. It was growing lighter with every passing second. Off to the west a coyote trotted out on a rocky ledge and barked a matutinal greeting to the sun god. As though worked on wires, the great golden orb swung up into the sky, and every crag and outcropping stood revealed in forbidding grandeur. Halfway up the slope the sunlight glinted on a rifle barrel that projected over the lip of the depression in which Morgan and his cohorts had spent the night. Nothing could be seen of the men on the rim. Jim was equally sure that his own bunch was not visible from above.

Without exposing himself he cupped his hand to his mouth and yelled, "This is your last chance to surrender, Morgan! Either walk out with your hands up or take the consequences!"

A cracking of rifles from the pocket was his answer. Hard on the heels of it came a rattle of gunfire from the rim.

"All right, boys," Jim muttered, "pick off every man that shows himself."

The firing continued in that fashion for half an hour or more without changing the situation appreciably. Jim had another man go down, the wound more serious this time. He didn't know how Morgan's crowd was faring, but it seemed unlikely that all of them had escaped the hail of slugs directed at the pocket.

Jim gave the word to edge up a bit. Taking advantage of every boulder and outcropping, the lower posse advanced a foot or two at a time. Presently from the rim there came an unexpected diversion. Three men dashed into the open, making for a ledge to the left of the quarry. Jim identified them easily enough—Oats, Wild Bill, and Curry. He couldn't hold back a groan as he saw the redhead go down. Mullhall stopped to pick him up and was dropped in his tracks. Curry made it, and from the safety of the ledge had the pocket at his mercy. His rifle began to buck, and the trapped men had to hug the ground. In that interval Wild Bill struggled to his feet and dragged Oats behind the ledge. In a few moments three rifles were cracking from that spot.

"Thank heaven!" Jim muttered. "All three of them are still able to pump a gun!"

In the pocket someone held up a rifle with a dirty handkerchief attached to the barrel and waved it back and forth in token of surrender.

"Okay!" Jim shouted. "Come out with your hands in the air!"

Steve Gore came first, followed by seven others. Three of them were bloodstained.

"Where's the rest of you?" Jim demanded.

"Duke and Morgan and Slip are done for!" Gore called back. "They can't make it!"

"All right, the eight of you walk this way!" To

his men Jim said, "This may be a trick. Look out for it."

Gore and the others were searched for hidden weapons and placed under guard.

"I'm going up to the pocket by myself," Jim said. "You boys keep me covered as best you can."

"You don't know what you're walking into," Dan protested. "I'll go with you."

"I'll go alone," Jim reiterated soberly. He set his rifle against a boulder, saying, "If I need a gun I'll be a lot faster with a forty-five."

Without exposing himself unnecessarily he climbed the slope. Out of the corner of his eye he saw Cass Curry leave the security of the ledge and move toward the pocket with him.

They got there almost together. Slip Egan lay huddled face down on the rock floor and in that stiff, grotesque fashion that only the dead have. Duke Legrand, so grievously wounded that his shirt was a wet red smear, had dragged himself to one side of the pocket and propped his shoulders against it. Morgan was sitting up, but he was obviously in bad shape, too.

"Cass, jump in there and gather up their guns," the sheriff called across to Curry. That accomplished, he stepped into the pocket himself, and the first thing he did was to ask Curry for Legrand's pistol. The latter looked on with narrowed, hate-ridden eyes. He had lost none of his sneering truculence. Jim's attention focused on him presently.

"Looks like you win, Mr. Sheriff," said Legrand. "No matter how smart you play things, a damn fool can throw you. If I'd shoved a gun into Chuck Silvey's belly the first time I saw him and pulled the trigger we wouldn't have ended up this way."

"Well, you got around to it eventually, Duke," Jim observed. "No question about that, is there?"

"None!"

"Then you got Kize, too. Corbett's been comparing the slugs he extracted. Both came from the same gun."

"So what?" Legrand muttered. "The old boy knew too much. A man does a lot of things when he's sparrin' for time. I'd thank you for a cigarette."

Curry rolled one for him, put it between the man's lips, and struck a light.

"Doc's with us," Jim said. "I'll get him up here."

"Don't bother on my account," Legrand returned. "Mebbe Morgan could use him. My number's up; no sawbones is goin' to do me any good."

A sharp warning yelp from Curry swung the sheriff around. Morgan had a second gun. If he had had strength enough left to whip it up quickly he could not have failed to send a bullet

230

crashing into Jim. In the second that was his the latter fired, and the stubby, blue-nosed .38 went flying out of Con's shattered hand.

"I used to think you had brains, Morgan," said Jim. "That was a long time ago. You haven't got sense enough to know the jig is up even now."

"Get Corbett!" Con howled, wringing his hand. "Don't let me die here!"

Jim called the doctor up and also waved the men in from the rim. Before Dan joined them Curry nudged the sheriff and pointed to Legrand. Duke was dead, the lighted cigarette still pasted to his lifeless lips.

"He's gone—and he ain't the only one," Curry said, his face hard and bitter.

Jim gave him a questioning glance.

"Bill," Curry informed him. "He kicked off without a whimper. I knew he was hurt bad. I fired a couple shots and turned to speak to him. He was glassy-eyed."

"What about Oats?" Jim's mouth was tight, fearful of Curry's answer.

"He was alive when I left him. But he's hurt bad, too."

Dan was there by then. Jim told him about Oats.

"Take a quick look at Morgan, and then we'll get over to the ledge."

"You're pretty well shot up, Con, but you'll

live," Corbett remarked after a hasty examination. He hurried after Jim then.

They found Oats unconscious. A slug had entered his chest, and the wound looked desperately serious to Jim.

"I don't believe it is," said Dan. "The bullet struck a rib and followed it around. I can feel the slug lodged against his spine. The pain's so great it has brought on a nervous collapse. We'll have to get him to town as quickly as we can."

"You think he'll be all right when the slug's removed?"

"I don't know," Dan replied reluctantly. "He'll live, but whether he'll be paralyzed or not I can't say. We'll have to carry him and Morgan as far as the Ford. We can get a wagon there. You call up some of the men, Jim."

After that was done they turned to Wild Bill. Dan closed the dead man's eyes.

"He came through for you at the end," he said.

"He sure did," Jim agreed. "It's like you said— there was good stuff in Bill. All it had to do was get to the surface."

Half an hour later the posse began moving down the Bend, herding its prisoners and carrying the dead and wounded. The few miners who were working quit their labors to watch them pass. Jim's thoughts were close to the surface. Corbett read them correctly.

"The diggings are shot," he said. "A lot of men have pulled out."

"Yeh, the camp's folding," Jim agreed. "A handful may stick it out until snow flies. That'll wind it up for keeps."

There was a crowd at Montero's store composed largely of men who were leaving the camp. Johnnie was excited and garrulous as usual. He supplied a wagon and horses, and the posse moved on to the temporary bridge at Misery Creek, where some delay was unavoidable. It didn't improve Morgan's chances. There was some irony in the fact that he had ordered the wrecking of the old bridge.

News of the posse's coming and what it had accomplished ran ahead of its arrival. Otis Longyear was waiting on the courthouse steps when Jim passed. He insisted on a word with him at once. After bringing him up to date on what had happened Jim said, "It's all yours now, Otis. It will take you to Congress if you play your cards right. It's too bad Rock Creek is without a newspaper."

"It's unthinkable!" Otis exclaimed. "The most important news this town ever had and no newspaper to print it! A newspaper is a necessity!"

"It sure is for anyone with political ambitions," Jim said with a thin smile.

"I'll see Messenger at once," the district attorney announced, ignoring the dig. "I'll ask him for an order enabling the *Enterprise* to continue publication under the jurisdiction of the court. Where will I find you in an hour?"

"I'll be at Dan's place. I'm going to stick close to it, too, until I know how Oats is going to fare."

"I'll bring the order there. You can persuade Iris to get the paper out, can't you?"

"I don't know how she'll feel about it. I'm willing to try."

On the way into town Oats had regained consciousness several times. After a few minutes he always blacked out again, and mercifully so, according to Dan. The operation to remove the slug was not a major one. When the anesthetic wore off and the redhead opened his eyes he found Jim at his bedside.

"How do you feel, Oats?"

"I feel fine. What you worryin' about?"

"Dan was afraid that slug might leave you paralyzed for life. Let's see you wiggle your toes." Oats obliged, and Jim said, "I guess you're all right."

"We sure cleaned 'em up, didn't we?" the red-haired one queried with a grin.

"Yeh, thanks to you and Bill. Listen, Oats, I've been here a couple hours and more. I haven't seen Iris. I've got some pressing business to discuss with her."

"Pressin', eh? I can imagine." Oats grinned broadly.

"That and something else," said Jim. "Longyear got a court order for her to go on publishing the paper. He was here with it an hour ago. He'll be back for his answer. I've got to see her. I'll be in again later."

He had been gone for better than half an hour when Otis walked in on Dan for the second time that morning.

"Been over there half an hour and not back yet?" the district attorney grumbled. "It's almost noon! I'll go on over myself. Maybe I can say something that'll swing her into line."

"Good heavens, no!" Dan declared emphatically. "If Jim can't persuade her, you couldn't. I believe you'll see her back at her desk in time to get out today's edition. Jim's got a good argument. He told me what he was going to say."

"He did?" Otis echoed eagerly.

"He's going to appeal to her pride in the town. Rock Creek is going to need her more than ever if she wants to keep it from going to pot. If I know her, that'll win her over. If she agrees to nothing more, she'll stay on until the trials are concluded and you've sent Morgan and the rest of them to the pen. She'll want to get away then for four to five weeks, and so will Jim."

"Together?"

"Certainly."

"Getting married, eh?"

"What's so surprising about that?" Dan demanded sharply. "Young people usually get married when they're as much in love with each other as Jim and Iris."

Will Ermine was a pseudonym for Harry Sinclair Drago, born in 1888 in Toledo, Ohio. Drago quit Toledo University to become a reporter for the Toledo *Bee*. He later turned to writing fiction with *Suzanna: A Romance of Early California*, published by Macauley in 1922. In 1927 he was in Hollywood, writing screenplays for Tom Mix and Buck Jones. In 1932 he went East, settling in White Plains, New York, where he concentrated on writing Western fiction for the magazine market, above all for Street & Smith's *Western Story Magazine*, to which he had contributed fiction as early as 1922. Many of his novels, written under the pseudonyms Bliss Lomax and Will Ermine, were serialised prior to book publication in magazines. Some of the best of these were also made into films. The Bliss Lomax titles *Colt Comrades* (Doubleday, Doran, 1939) and *The Leather Burners* (Doubleday, Doran, 1940) were filmed as superior entries in the Hopalong Cassidy series with William Boyd, *Colt Comrades* (United Artists, 1943) and *Leather Burners* (United Artists, 1943). At his best Drago wrote Western stories that are tightly plotted with engaging characters, and often it is suspense that comprises their pulse and dramatic pacing.

Center Point Large Print
600 Brooks Road / PO Box 1
Thorndike, ME 04986-0001 USA

(207) 568-3717

US & Canada:
1 800 929-9108
www.centerpointlargeprint.com

melville
K6